MW00770026

SHE WHO KNOWS

DAW Books proudly presents
the novels of Nnedi Okorafor

WHO FEARS DEATH

THE BOOK OF PHOENIX

NOOR

BINTI: THE COMPLETE TRILOGY

(Binti | Binti: Home | Binti: The Night Masquerade
with Binti: Sacred Fire)

The Desert Magician's Duology

SHADOW SPEAKER (Book 1)

LIKE THUNDER (Book 2)

She Who Knows

SHE WHO KNOWS (Book 1)

SHE WHO KNOWS: ONE-WAY WITCH (Book 2)

SHE WHO KNOWS

BOOK ONE

NNEDI OKORAFOR

DAW BOOKS
New York

Jacket illustration by Greg Ruth

Jacket design by Jim Tierney

Edited by Betsy Wollheim

DAW Book Collectors No. 1964

DAW Books
An imprint of Astra Publishing House
dawbooks.com
DAW Books and its logo are registered trademarks of
Astra Publishing House

Printed in the United States of America

Library of Congress Cataloging-in-Publication Data
is available upon request

ISBN 9780756418953 (hardcover) | ISBN 9780756418960 (ebook)

First edition: August 2024
10 9 8 7 6 5 4 3 2 1

Dedicated to those women who were told or made
to feel their voices were incendiary.

Author's Note

I've wanted to write Najeeba's story for years. *Who Fears Death* was originally two novels, a Book 1 and a Book 2, and I wrote about Najeeba in the first. Most of her parts of the story never made it into the published singular novel. However, those kernels of story stayed with me, and they were so strong that over the years, I found myself speaking about Najeeba as if I'd already told her story.

To understand this novella, there are some things you need to know: Najeeba's amazing and intense daughter Onyesonwu did something . . . big. The world has changed, realigned. Najeeba helped her daughter accomplish this feat. If you want to know the story of how it happened, you'll find it in *Who Fears Death*, a novel named after its titular character, Onyesonwu (her name literally means the question: "Who Fears Death?"). However, those natural abilities Najeeba used to help her daughter Onyesonwu were not new. They had their own origin long before Onyesonwu was born. This novella is *that* story.

Other things to know: The Okeke people are people of African descent. The Nuru people are of Arab descent. The Earth of this story is our distant future Earth, so there will be some things you recognize blended with things you don't. There are always consequences, results, fruitions, and descendants, just as there are ancestors. If you need a precise longitude and latitude, go with 12.8628° N, 30.2176° E.

Salt, dust, wind, and a powerful will—this is Najeeba's tale.

Nnedi

SHE WHO KNOWS

"When you come out of the storm,
you won't be the same person who walked in."

—*Haruki Murakami*, Kafka on the Shore

CHAPTER 1

Onye Fulu Mmo Di?

[Who Sees a Spirit and Lives?]

If I stood there long enough, I was sure I'd see one of the Old Ones dancing in the distance. That's how hot it was that day. I brought my portable from my pocket and looked at it. At the top of the screen, it announced it was the hottest day of the year. Then it decided to shut itself down for the next hour to keep from overheating.

It was dusk, yet still boiling hot outside. Not unusual, but a little disturbing nonetheless. A thin shower of rain began to fall and a large brown bird squawked and then took to the air from the neighbor's roof across the road. The desert is strange.

I was standing there because this was the moment. The beginning. I shut my eyes and took a deep breath, inhaling it all, the fact of it. Through my mouth, to my lungs, to the rest of my body.

I'd just come from my brother's house, where I'd

spent some hours with their new baby who was so fat and cute and happy. I'd been thinking about what it would be like for me in a few years. Now I wasn't thinking about any of that at all. My mind was full of a new knowledge.

I turned around, opened the door, and went inside to find my parents. I was thirteen years old and I was a girl. Yet I was *sure*. Absolutely positive. I opened my eyes and paused, rubbing my forehead.

"I can't believe this," I whispered. I went inside and found my mother in the kitchen, where she usually was at this time of day.

"Fry those yams, Najeeba," she said, her back to me. The round slices were on the cutting board and the deep pan of oil on the stove was just starting to heat up. On the other burner was another large pan of sizzling chopped tomatoes, olive oil, smoked aku, sautéed onions, curry, smoked mushrooms, and chili peppers. On the counter behind her, sitting in its own sunbeam on its royal blue ornate plate with the gold flecks embedded into the shiny porcelain, was a large cube of salt. The bowl of several stirred eggs was on the counter beside the stove. Mama was making egg stew. I joined her, my heart pounding hard. I opened my mouth to speak. To ask.

Then my father entered the kitchen, grinning. He put his arms around my mother.

"Papa, I want to go this year, too," I blurted.

My parents stared at me, and then my mother turned and looked at Papa. "You've told our daughter before me?" she asked.

"No," he said, looking questioningly at me. "I haven't told anyone. I was about to tell *you* right now."

Mama looked hard at me with her near-black piercing eyes. "What does it feel like?" she asked.

I thought for a moment. I'd never asked Papa, so I had no context to draw from. I said the first thing that came to mind: "Like . . . like the wind is blowing me toward the door."

Mama's eyes grew wide and she looked at Papa, who also looked shocked. Then she grinned. "I've given birth to *three* boys, not two."

"Apparently so," Papa agreed.

Mama hugged me tightly, kissed my cheek, and then she shoved me back toward the now-sizzling yams. But I noticed her eyes had grown wet. She loved her solitude, but she didn't want me to go. She stepped to the cube of salt and picked it up.

"Salt is life," the three of us softly recited as she grated some into the bowl of eggs.

My father and I held out our hands and my mother grated some onto them. We rubbed our hands together and then pressed them to our chests. Salt has always been important to humanity, yes. Even here in Jwahir, it's worth more than most things. But back in my village, salt was sacred to my people. It was life but also culture, self-worth, our purpose for existing.

My mother poured the egg into the sizzling vegetables and began to slowly turn it. Papa sat at the table, looking hard at me as he continued to rub his hands. "You're sure?"

"Yes, Papa."

"It's a week there, a week to the market, a week back."

"I know," I said.

"The way is not easy."

"I know, Papa."

"The Okeke at the market are camelshit people," Mama added. "They see us as abominations, even if you are kind. Doesn't matter that we are *all* Okeke people. It is the plight of being Osu-nu."

"I know, Mama."

"You'll still have to be kind, but strong."

I nodded. "Yes, Mama."

"Is your Abdul strong enough?" Papa asked. Abdul was my camel.

"I will make him so," I said.

I turned to look at the frying yam as Mama looked to my father and my father to my mother and they did that silent thing they always did. My parents could have a whole complicated conversation without opening their mouths.

My oldest brother, Rayan, said they spoke through their eyes, but it was more than that. When they talked like this, I always wanted to leave because it just made me feel so . . . not there. Like they'd already shoved me out of the room and shut the door and my body just had to catch up with my spirit. But I stayed where I was, letting the yams brown and then flipping them over. I carefully took them out, stacking them on the cloth-covered plate.

Mama gave the egg stew a few more turns and ladled it all into a large bowl. The stew was fluffy and hot and I had no doubt that it was tasty. With the yams, it was the perfect meal. "Who will maintain our vegetable garden while you're away, Najeeba?" my mother asked me, preparing a plate of the stew and yams for my father.

"You will, Mama," I said.

"No," she said, smirking. "I will pay someone to do it."

The three of us laughed. Of course she would.

━━━

We Osu-nu live in villages built away from other Okeke peoples. All our villages have the same name, Adoro. My village is Adoro 5. Aro, you *know* the story of my people. Your clan resides not far from mine and I'm sure you never traveled near us. Am I right?

To your clan, even though we look just like you, we are to be avoided. It's forbidden to befriend or marry us. Osu-nu people are untouchable Okeke people; we are the slaves who chose to be slaves to the goddess Adoro so that we could be free. You only know the depth of the story as it is shared amongst your people. That's not the full story, but I won't get into that today. I need to open other doors for you first.

My father named me Najeeba. It means "She who knows." He chose it out of a list of ten names my mother presented to him the day before she gave birth to me. I'm only now beginning to understand why he may have chosen that name. It definitely suits me. It is what many call a "freedom name." What the Osu-nu people are most known for, aside from the legend of how we forced our freedom and enslavement, is salt. You cannot survive these lands, these times, without salt. Water is life, but salt is to live. What is blood without salt in it? How can you look at the desert and not understand that surviving in it depends on salt?

From what we tell ourselves, the origin of the *prosperous* Osu-nu started with two Osu-nu women traveling together who found the ghost of the lake. They were fleeing something (some say from their own village clan, which would make them outcasts of outcasts), and they had been traveling for a long time. They were searching for the end of everything. Their camels died, but they had their own feet, and their sandals were well made. They had equipment and supplies, which they carried. And they had each other. So they continued on into the unknown deserts.

Somehow, maybe by their own sheer will and outrage, these two women lived. And at some point, while walking during a night brightened by a full moon, they stepped onto land that cracked beneath their feet. Salt. They made camp here and went to sleep.

When the sun came up, it was as if they stood

before the border of another planet. They had to shield their eyes, for the desert sun reflected brightly off the surface of the salt. Shards of it erupted from the earth. There were large and tiny perfect cubes of it scattered as far as the eye could see. A land of salt crystals.

The two women could not believe their eyes. The doom they felt for their lives dissipated. They'd fled towns and villages of Okeke where salt was the sparsest and therefore most valued item. Even in the cities, where both had vowed to never ever go, salt was a great commodity. One had to merely travel in this direction for months, giving up on life, yet somehow living and surviving on nothing but what one could carry.

It was a dead lake. A vast body of water that the goddess Ani had killed when she turned back to the Earth and saw what the dark-skinned Okeke people were doing. She'd then brought the lighter-skinned Nuru people from the stars. When Ani had made the world desert, this lake had evaporated instantly and left all that had given it life. Just like the caves full of computers, places like this were mentioned in the Great Book. But unlike the caves full of computers that many have found since, the two women were the first to find a dead lake.

They stayed in that place for a while. And when they were ready, they packed up, bringing two of the largest, clearest cubes of salt they could find. Cubes so pure that they were like frozen lake water that did not melt in the sun. The two women eventually brought the cubes to a town that did not know them. They sold them for more money than a camel. And this was the start of a lucrative Osu-nu business, for the women made it known that they were Osu-nu and only their own people would work with them.

The narrative of how only an Osu-nu, enslaved to the goddess Adoro, could survive the journey to the dead to retrieve the salt of life solidified into fact. Over the years, decades, centuries, the salt roads, an intuitive path to the dead lake, formed and strengthened, and the success of the Osu-nu people was sealed.

And as those two women grew their business, the first rule they set as they brought in others was that no group went to harvest from the place at the same time. There was always someone who was coming and going, arriving and leaving and so the salt roads remained uncongested.

And there was another reason why others left the Osu-nu to retrieve the salt. Though quiet, the salt roads were indeed . . . occupied. No one dared to put a name to who or what occupied them, but everyone knew that whoever or whatever it was was not kind. And when Okeke who were not Osu-nu tried to travel the salt roads, they never returned. And so it was Osu-nu men who traveled the salt roads to collect salt, which they then sold in the open Okeke markets and even at some of the Nuru markets. And each man who headed a caravan would wake up at a specific time each year *knowing* it was time to go. No one knew how this system worked, but it did. Ask my father and he would have told you that in all his times traveling there, he never ever met up with another caravan.

My father had been doing this all my life, and my brothers Rayan and Ger, who were twenty-seven and twenty-five years old, had been going since they were teens. I was thirteen and I'd grown up in a household hearing their stories about the profound Knowing when to go, what dwelled on the salt roads, the journey, the markets.

There was always this spice of mysticism to it all. I recognized the touch of spirits and ancestors. It was legend to me. It was legend to all my agemates, really. Traveling the salt roads was the stuff of grown men. A few of the older boys who were thirteen and fourteen were starting to go and they walked around like small kings. And now, *I* was going to be the first girl to go.

But first, I had to see to my garden. My mother was right to think of it. I was good with plants, always had been. What started off as me playing around when I was about five years old had become a full-grown garden complete with tomatoes, chili peppers, onions, cactus candy, and yams, that I'd rigged with an irrigation system connected to an automated capture station and shading I'd constructed to protect some of the more sensitive plants from the harsh sun during dry season. It took up all of our backyard and much of my time.

The surplus I harvested made a good amount of money for the family. Between my father's salt business, my brothers working for the business, my mother's writing services, and my garden, we did well enough that much of what was made went to my savings and spending money, which I didn't really need.

I was digging around some of the tomatoes, aerating the soil, when I heard, "Najeeeeeeeba! Always with her butt to the sky."

I blinked for a moment, coming back to myself. I'd been so focused on what I was doing that the sound of my best friend's voice was jarring. I sat up, shading my eyes against the bright sun. "Peter!" I grinned. "I was coming to see you when I finished this."

She put her hands up. "Not like *that*, I hope." She was wearing an all-white dress that brought out the rich darkness of her skin. She was clearly going to the Paper House. I wriggled my dirty hands at her and she took a step back. I giggled and asked, "What are you looking for there?"

"You didn't hear? There was a fresh haul last night. Two camels came carrying *five* chests." Peter could read way better than I ever could, but like all the girls in my village, I loved going to the Paper House, too. Boys who traveled the salt roads and made their fortune at the markets didn't think poring over ancient found documents and books was a good use of time. Most of the scholars who went to the Paper House were women and girls. It didn't help that in order to enter the Paper House, you had to wear all white, make sure you were super clean beforehand, be subjected to in-spection and additional decontamination when you arrived there, and treat every document like a new-born baby.

"I've been in my garden all morning, as you can see," I said.

"You want to meet me there in an hour? I'm going to be there all day."

"I would . . . but I can't now." I smiled and got up. "I mean . . . okay, I have something amazing to tell you!"

"What? Is everything okay with Obi?"

I paused and frowned. I'd forgotten about Obi, the boy I'd become intimate with over the last two months. "Oh . . . no, no, it's not about him." I took a deep breath and then blurted, "I'm . . . I'm going with my papa and brothers on the salt roads this year!"

"Wait . . . what?"

I grinned bigger. "Even my mother says it's okay."

"But . . . what about . . . you'll be gone for almost two months!"

We stared at each other for a moment. Peter suddenly laughed. "You're joking."

"No," I said. "I'm not. I'm going."

"You're not a man," she said, cocking her head.

"No. I'm not."

"Then how?"

"Because I want to. I knew it was time to leave *before* my father said anything."

She frowned hard at me. "Doesn't matter. You're a girl. Girls and women don't go on the salt roads."

"Says who?" I was getting angry now.

"You're really serious."

"Yes! I've always wanted to go. You know that."

"I thought you were just talking garbage."

I hadn't been serious because I didn't think it was possible. But I'd dreamed of it as people dream of flying or staying young forever. Peter knew that because I talked about it all the time. "Peter, I'm going on the salt roads with my father and brothers. We leave in about two weeks. I can't go to the Paper House with you because I have to start getting ready today. Starting with my camel Abdul."

Peter stared at me and I stared right back. I knew what she was thinking and I hated it: *Why don't you grow out your hair and wear beautiful dresses? You look like a boy.* I didn't look like a boy at all. I was tall, lean. Puberty had not really arrived for me yet, but so what? And I preferred to wear my hair shaved close; less trouble, plus it looked nice on me. I often wore the large glass hoop earrings and bracelets my mother had given me on my eleventh birthday, too.

"Do whatever you like," Peter said. She turned and started walking away.

"You don't want me to go?" I pressed.

She turned around. "I want you to be able to find a husband when the time comes. You're my best friend. I want the best for you. Always."

"I want to go, Peter. I really do."

She shrugged and walked away. I watched her go, a weight of sadness pulling at my belly. I reached up with my dirty hand and ran it over my short hair. Then I dug my hand into the soil and I felt better, a bit. A few minutes later, tears fell from my eyes, mixing with the soil.

━━━━

The next day, I went to find Obi. Where I was a tall, lean thirteen-year-old with near-black smooth skin, Obi was a short thirteen-year-old with equally smooth dark skin and the kindest smile I'd ever seen. And Obi *saw* me. A year ago, he'd come up to me at school and told me, "You can cut your hair and wear those boy clothes, but I still *see* you, Najeeba. You are beautiful."

A twelve-year-old boy said this. No one had been around us in that moment and I'd just looked at him, stunned. And he was so much shorter than me, but he'd looked me right in the eye. No one had ever been so sincere. He'd smiled that kind smile and then walked away, so sure of himself that he didn't wait for my response. We became friends. Me, Obi, Peter, and our friend Europe. Then Obi and I shared a kiss one day. Then later more kisses. He made me feel so special and he loved listening to me talk.

I found him now playing football on the outskirts of town with some other boys. He was one of the best players, and I sat down and watched him play for nearly a half hour before he noticed me. He jogged over. He was sweaty and dusty. Happy.

"Naj," he said, sitting beside me and taking the cup of water I'd been sipping from. He drank it all and said, "I thought you'd be in the Paper House."

"Peter's mad at me. Figured I'd come see you instead."

"What's she mad about? Did you get dirt on her white dress?"

"Something like that," I said. "Listen, Peter. I'm going on the salt roads. I asked my papa yesterday and he said yes."

Obi stood up, frowning deeply. "You . . . can't do that."

"I am."

"*I* haven't even gone with *my* father yet."

"So?"

"But you're a girl."

"There's no rule that says girls can't—"

"Ah," he said, holding up a finger. "Ah, I see why Peter is angry with you. You can't go, Naj. You have to know that."

"I am going." I pulled my long legs to my chest and pressed my face to my thighs. I couldn't stop the hurt, surprised tears from welling up in my eyes.

"You aren't."

"I am!" I screamed into my legs.

"What about me?"

"What about you?" I said, looking at him. "I'll be gone a month and a half. Are you going somewhere?"

He groaned, grabbing his short dreadlocks in both fists. "Okay. Fine! Go, then." He ran back to the football game. Over his shoulder, he shouted, "I won't be with a girl who thinks she's a boy!"

The next two weeks were hard for me. It was school break, which meant no school until I got back. Neither Peter nor Obi would speak to me. So I spent the entire time alone in my garden or preparing my camel Abdul. My mother was busy with her writing, as always.

My father was busy organizing his supplies and schedules, and my brothers had left a week before us to scout for business at the market before we all set out. They would meet us on the way.

So no one noticed that I was sad. I wasn't trying to be a boy. I wasn't trying to look like a boy. I wasn't trying to do what boys did. I wanted to be with my father and I wanted to travel on the salt roads. I'd woken up that day knowing it was time and sure that I should go, too. But my friends saw and felt something else. Everyone seemed to see and feel something else.

My mother didn't tell any of her friends I was going, nor did my father. When the day came, neither Peter nor Obi came to see me off. To people in my town, I'd just disappear, as girls often did. We were sent to live in other towns to help relatives with housework and child care, to have unwanted babies, to study at a non-Osu-nu university, and most commonly to be a concubine in a non-Osu-nu marriage. I didn't worry too much about what people would think . . . I worried only about my friends. I wished Peter and Obi could see things from my perspective. They knew me best, they should have understood.

As I climbed onto Abdul, I fought off my fatigue. I'd cried myself to sleep the night before. I was lonely, I was suddenly unsure of everything, and I was leaving.

"You ready?" my father asked.

"Yes, Papa."

He nodded, patting Abdul's neck. "He is full of water, his hump full of fat stores, his body full of rest. You did a good job with him," he said.

"She is her mother's daughter," my mother said. She sipped from her glass of palm wine, a strange drink for so early in the morning. I wondered if she was a bit drunk.

"She is," my father said. "Come here, my love."

My mother came around his camel, whose name was Dusty, and stood looking up at him. They stayed like that for several moments, doing their silent conversation thing. I patted Abdul on the neck and looked up at the sky. The sun hadn't warmed it yet, but there wasn't a cloud in sight. I wore my weather-treated veil around my neck, but I knew I'd have to wrap it around my head in a few hours. The long-sleeved top and pants I wore were also weather-treated, and my portable would stay in my pocket once the sun was up. The sun could do whatever it wanted; I was ready for it.

My mother took my father's hand, and he bent down and kissed hers. "I expect you to choose a fine camel for me. Not one scruffy and uncouth like Dusty." She patted my father's camel longingly.

"I will find you a beautiful camel that will make Yeleen proud."

Yeleen was my mother's old camel who'd died six months ago after a long life as one of my mother's best friends. We were all glad that my mother finally decided to come out of mourning and open herself to a new one. Mama stepped back and slapped Dusty's rump, and the camel groaned dramatically, making us all laugh. "Off you go," she said. Dusty began walking, Abdul following his lead.

"Until I return," my father recited. I wanted to say it, too. He always said the same thing when he left, and it felt odd being on the leaving side this time. We started up the road, walking slowly. I turned around and waved at my mother. She waved back, laughing. "My daughter, enjoy your adventures!"

"I will, Mama! I will!"

A few people greeted my father and wished him well as we made our way out of the village. No one paid any attention to me. Most likely, they assumed I was seeing him off and would return after going with him a few miles. Wives, daughters, and female friends often did that, though my mother and I never had.

We passed homes, gardens, repair shops that weren't open yet, the market, which was bustling with activity already, the town square. I could see a hint of the Paper House on the other side of the village, a large white stone building. I wondered if Peter was already in there, getting some reading done in the early morning as she sometimes liked to do. In my head, I did not say goodbye to her or to Obi. *I'll see them when I get back*, I thought as we finally passed the last home on the edge of the village.

Sun. Sun. Sun. But it was no problem. My clothes protected me, keeping me cool, while being lightweight and silky. I kept my portable in my pocket; it would have overheated and shut itself down on its own if I hadn't. Still, I played some old Afrobeats tunes that I had stored. My father preferred to listen to the Great Book, but there was plenty of time for that.

Personally, I'd never had much of an attachment to the Great Book. It was a book about a world and a people that couldn't even imagine me, let alone include me. Everyone in the Great Book had a role, a position, assigned because of anything but who they were. And then there was the way that darker-skinned people were shown as *less than*. I didn't know why my parents accepted it, why so *many* accepted it. Nevertheless, I never told my father my thoughts on the subject, of course. Or my mother, who also loved reading the Great Book.

My papa and I did not speak much as we traveled. Our camels had more to say, groaning and grumbling at each other. Both my father and the camels seemed to know instinctively which way to go. The moment we left the town limits, it was just the four of us and open sky. We passed the rocky ridges, and then came the miles and miles of sand dunes. We camped hours later on a flat swath of hardpan.

"Well?" my father asked as we lay on our mats before the fire we'd built.

"My butt hurts," I said.

"It'll get stronger."

I groaned, rubbing my tailbone. "So how do you know where to meet Rayan and Ger? I know you have coordinates, but I haven't seen you look at your portable all day and you don't like to use audio."

"Today was hot. To bring it out would only make it shut down in the heat."

"So how do you know where to go?"

"I know the coordinates and I can read them up here." He tapped his forehead.

"In your mind? You can map in your mind?"

"Yes, my dear. You know this."

"Well, at home. But I didn't know you could . . . do it for this far."

He lay back and shut his eyes. "We will meet your brothers tomorrow. Probably in the evening. Then it will be some days to the ghost lake. Get some sleep." He turned over and was quiet.

I lay there for a while, listening to the desert. It was a hot night, so the desert creatures were vibrating at a high frequency. Crickets chirped, a desert fox yipped in the distance, maybe what could have been an owl screeched, and . . . the stars above. I took a sip of the cup of water beside me. The liquid cooled my throat as it traveled down to my stomach. Papa's capture station whooshed as it pulled down a coil of moisture from the clouds. A blast of cool air rolled over our small camp. I heard Abdul softly sigh with pleasure.

I felt cool and then light, and I let my eyes focus on the cloud that the capture station was pulling from. Behind it was the ghostly haze of the Milky Way, something I'd grown up seeing. I relaxed as my sleep mat felt soft, then cool, then thick, as if I were rising slowly off the ground.

Higher and higher. I closed my eyes and fell asleep.

━━━

I awoke to the sound of Dusty gleefully rolling in the dust. I turned to watch the camel demonstrate how he got his name. Abdul was nearby, drowsily watching Dusty like he was the most ridiculous thing he'd ever seen. I smiled and slowly got up.

"A good sign," my father said. He was already up, using a bucket of water to wash his face and brush his teeth. "I didn't have to wake you. You must have slept well."

I nodded. I felt great. I stretched my back. My first night in the desert. The sun was still hours away. The potential of the day was almost tangible. We were up and moving within a half hour. It wasn't hot enough for my weather-treated veil or shirt, so I wore a tank top. I held my arms out as Abdul followed Dusty at a brisk pace. My backside still hurt, but not much . . . yet.

My father played the Great Book, and as the sun rose, I frowned as the rough male voice told us about the "black-skinned" Okeke people deciding to make the worst decisions humankind has ever made. Africans and their technology and their need to play God. My father recited the words along with the recording, sometimes laughing at parts and other times raising an index finger to proclaim other parts. I zoned out, staring at the sand dunes. They were soft, eternally folding over themselves.

I was wrapping my face with my weather-treated veil around my head when I saw the witch. I gasped, pulling Abdul's reins. I don't know how it took me that long to see it, because it was so close. My father must have seen it a while ago, because he said, "It will not bother us as long as we don't bother it." He looked back at me. "Come on, daughter. Leave her be."

It spiraled high into the sky, over a quarter of a mile up, softly twisting and swirling dust and sand like water. It didn't sound like roaring the way I always imagined a witch would sound up close like this. It sounded like someone's mother telling me to be quiet. To be quiet and listen.

I was off my camel before I knew what I was going to do. Some of the sand flipped into my sandals as my feet hit the warm sands.

"Jeeb! What are you doing!" my father shouted.

"I just want to see," I said. "Papa, it's harmless,

right? I've never seen a witch up close." It churned up the sand dune before us. A miniature tornado, it reminded me of the coil of air and water vapor that extended from capture stations when they were pulling from the clouds above.

"They are not as weak as they look," my father shouted. He was still on his camel. "Leave it alone!"

Shhhhhhhhhhhhh! it proclaimed.

I ran to it. Do not ask me why. I don't *know* why. It was one of those things. They say that before you are twenty years old, your brain is not fully formed yet, and because of this, you make brash impulsive nonsense decisions. I was running from my father and our camels to throw my arms around a witch. As I got closer and closer, my mind kept asking, *What are you doing?*

What are you doing? Stop! Stop! I didn't stop.

"Jeeb!" my father shouted.

The witch seemed to pause just as I got to it. Churning sand and dust. The sound of an inhaling god. The slap of sand on my face. On my exposed hands. The whoosh of air over my short hair. The witch took me. I glanced down just in time to see my feet leave the ground.

How is this possible? I thought, the breath sucked from my lungs. Up. The witch yanked me into the air.

Aro, this was another moment. *This* was the switch when it flipped up. On. You asked me when it began. My sleep the night before was a hint. There were other times before that, too. All of them wispy like vapor. Moisture, but not rain. *This* was rain. Rain before the full thunderstorm.

My father says the witch lifted and took me at least twenty feet up into its body. By the time he got to me, the witch had set me back down and retreated back into the sky. I don't remember much more than wind, noise, and a glimpse of something red-orange I couldn't put words to. But I did recall a brief moment where everything stopped, there was blue sky, and all I could hear was the wind.

Then I felt pain and was looking into Papa's face.

"Jeeb?" he asked.

"Papa!" I blinked sand and dust from my eyes. I sat up and winced. My face hurt. The dust had sanded away a thin layer of the skin on the left side of my face, my left arm, and my left leg. It stung horribly and some of the grains of sand were so embedded in my flesh that it would take days for them to make their way to the surface and fall out. But I still laughed. My father's face went from concerned to angry.

"Have you lost your mind?!" he shouted. He shook me a bit. "Why are you smiling?"

The air was still, the dust settled. Was I smiling? I turned to look where the witch had whirled and danced. I couldn't speak, I was so out of breath. And words would not come to me. The camels stood waiting in the distance. They knew never to approach a witch. "Get up," my father snapped, but he lifted me up before I could even try. "Stupid child!" But he was hugging me to him as he led me to the camels.

Abdul sniffed me and shook out his fur. My pants and shirt were encrusted with sand, and I changed out of them into the only other clothes I'd brought with me, a long orange dress with long sleeves. My father wiped my face, legs, and arms with water and then rubbed my face with coconut oil. "It could have killed you. It looked like it tried to. Imagine what kind of father I'd be! Did you even think about that?"

I should have felt terrible and selfish. I felt quiet. I wanted my father to stay near me, but not so close that I had to talk or that I could hear his frightened anger. I had words now, but I didn't feel like sharing them. I went to Abdul and he looked at me with great suspicion. I slowly reached up and patted his rough neck. He leaned away from me, but he stayed where he was.

I could hear my father talking on his portable to my mother. He wasn't talking about me. He was telling her we hadn't reached my brothers yet and that he missed her. He told her nothing about what had happened with the witch. A breeze picked up and I turned my head toward it, so that I couldn't hear my father speaking. It was hot, as the desert's breath always is at this time of the day. I wanted to tell the breeze that I was fine, but I still didn't want to speak. I kept the experience inside me for now. I was thirteen years old. Old enough to know when something liminal had just been revealed.

Three hours later, as the sun went down, we came to where my brothers Rayan and Ger were camped. They'd been traveling the salt roads for over ten years with my father. Thus, we could see their high-ceilinged, white goat-skinned tent with the red flag at the top from quite far away, and I could see both of them standing in front of it, waving.

I still hadn't explained anything to Papa and he

still seemed annoyed with me. I hoped that the excitement of meeting up with my brothers would overshadow what had happened to me. It seemed to, and thankfully, soon I was left alone to step away and sit on a sand dune as Papa and my brothers caught up and discussed the journey for tomorrow.

CHAPTER 2

Dead Lake

My brother Rayan thought he was on my father's level because he was almost thirty years old, married with three children, including a male newborn. Ger had married his wife months ago and all he wanted to do was chat with her on his portable the entire time, but also make as much money as possible so they could build on their house before having a baby. All of this added up to them being annoyed I was there.

"You should be home reading manuscripts, papers, and books at the Paper House and getting ready for your husband," Rayan said over his shoulder. His dusty red camel, whose name was Mars, liked to walk at the front, even ahead of my father. The beast was just as entitled as my brother.

"Didn't you hear Papa?" I said. "I *knew* when it was time to go. I had the calling."

"Not all calls are meant to be answered," Ger said. He was right beside me and I wanted to punch him.

"Exactly," Rayan said. "Girls aren't meant to be out here."

I looked behind me at my father for backup. He said nothing, only gazing back at me. I frowned and turned around.

"We are all here," my father said. "Let's all *be* here."

I said little else for the next many hours. It was tiring. I was there; why should I explain why? Why did my own brothers, who *liked* me, keep saying I should not be there? My father barely defended me. And all around me were miles and miles of desert, no human villages in sight. I let my mind travel to the witch, what I'd seen. I still had no urge to share my experience with any of them, not even with my father. He'd said nothing to my brothers, which made me not want to tell them even more.

I fell asleep on my camel. It was a talent that I had. When I look back, it all makes sense why I was able to do it. I could sit on my camel and sleep deeply without falling off. My brothers and father would say that I'd sway this way and that, but I'd never fall. My brother Rayan said it was as if I'd left a part of my-self behind to watch over my body, while the major-ity of me went elsewhere. So I did not know when we crested the sand dune. I heard my father say, "I never get used to it."

"It scares me," Ger said. "I described it once to Zora and she said that she never ever wanted to set eyes on this place. I understand."

"You two are made for each other. Two cowards," Rayan laughed.

Slowly, I opened my eyes. I'd been awake for a few minutes, but once I understood what I was about to see, I hesitated. Some part of me that had listened to all the words, sentiments of people, who had grown up amongst the Osu-nu, who believed the salt roads were for Osu-nu men only, despite the fact that they were discovered by two women, was certain that when I set eyes upon the ghost of the lake, I'd turn into a pillar of salt. There were documents shelved in the Paper House that said so. I'd read them myself with Peter last year and we'd thought it funny, be-cause we didn't think we had to worry about it ei-ther way.

I took a leap of faith. I opened my eyes wide. Then . . . I gasped. My father and brothers all turned to me. "See?" my father said, smiling. "The mere sight of it does not change her."

"What do you think, Najeeba?" Ger asked.

I took a few moments. Then I said, "The first to see this place were women," I said. "I'm probably thinking what they thought . . . that death sometimes creates great beauty."

The dead lake was the most beautiful and mysterious place I'd ever seen. Down the sand dune, the sand simply ended, and from horizon to horizon the land became salt. The Great Book spoke of Ani awakening and turning her attention back to the Earth, of her then pulling in the stars from which she plucked the Nuru people. Scholars and scientists said there was more to it. Seeing what I was seeing now, I agreed. The peaceful death of a lake could not have done all this. No.

It glistened and sparkled in the sunlight. My father and brothers had already put on their sunglasses and I put mine on now. Crystals, shards, large, medium, and small. More salt than humanity could ever consume. Most of it was murky with detritus, like dead leaves, seaweed, pebbles, dirt, other minerals, but some of it was clearer. Before Ani's return, the

Okeke people had used their twisted technology to strain salt from the sea to make it drinkable. That salt was sometimes dumped into lakes like this one. So there had already been an extremely high concentration of salt in the lake. Maybe while the lake was alive, it was also dead. But that still didn't explain what I was seeing. Ani had worked her juju here so long ago, and it was still so incredibly powerful.

"Ani is great," I whispered.

We set up camp on the top of the sand dune. When we finished, my father trudged up an even higher dune, where he just stood looking at the dead lake.

"What's he doing?" I asked my brother Rayan.

"It's how Papa always finds the rarest cubes of salt to sell. He goes up and looks right when we arrive. He says certain things stand out for him and that's where he goes to look."

"It works every time," Ger added. "Though he doesn't always know what kind of weird salt he'll find. Watch. Before we leave, he'll find something."

Papa stood up there for nearly an hour. When he came down, he said nothing, acting like what he'd done was perfectly normal. To my brothers, I guess, it was. Once we'd settled in a bit, we went to the dead lake. The camels were happy to stay behind. We left our mining equipment with them. We would start all that tomorrow.

"Does anything live here?" I asked.

"Not really," my father said. "Some birds come here to roost, but they find food elsewhere. Vultures come to prey on the ones who die while roosting."

The closer we got to the salt, the more surreal it seemed. We crossed an area that had obviously been mined. When you looked up, this barely left a dent in the miles and miles of crystals. Human beings would go extinct before the salt here ran out, no matter how much people came and took. When my brothers and father stopped to look at a particular salt cube, I turned the other way, toward the crystal wilderness.

"Ani is great," I whispered. In the distance, a cluster of cubes and shards glistened orange-yellow in the waning sunlight. As I stared at it, the light shifted, and I could have sworn I saw something long and lean rise from the salt. Or maybe it was just the heat. I snapped my fingers above my head to ward off the evil eye and turned back to Papa and my brothers, who'd decided the cube wasn't worth pulling up. Still, when we started walking, I looked back. The orange-yellow light was gone.

"This place is strange," I muttered.

We reached the thicker shards and cubes, my father tapping on each and gazing into them like an oracle gazing into a pool or water or mirror. My brothers did the same, but it was clear that my father knew better what to look and listen for than they did. Locating good salt was not just a skill, it was a talent. The ground cracked and shattered, leaving footprints. I found the sound and feel satisfying and I stamped my feet as I walked.

"Be serious," Rayan snapped.

"Why? What does it even matter?"

"Just have some respect," he said. "This place is sacred. It is the livelihood of our people."

I rolled my eyes, stamped one more foot, and then treaded lightly.

"It's her first time here," Ger said. "Don't act like you didn't do the same thing when it was you."

Up ahead, our father had stepped onto a large cube. He stood on it and looked down. The sun was shining through it so clearly that I had to shield my eyes. "Ah!

We are lucky. This is a *good* one," he said. "See how clear it is, Najeeba? Like ice. No detritus trapped inside, no dead creatures."

"*Kai!* Good find, Papa," Rayan said. "And we just got here!"

"There can be dead things in the salt?" I asked.

"Almost always, yes," he said. "This one is unusual." He knelt down and placed a solar flag on it. This would make it easy to locate tomorrow. "It's one of the ways we know this lake did not die naturally. It died fast . . . and hot."

I sat on a smaller cube, my brothers sitting on a shard and another cube. We stayed like that for a while, listening to the quiet. It wasn't the same type of quiet as the desert, which is a heavy, cleansing quiet that stills the soul. It was a frantic quiet, as if something was vibrating in privacy. The sun was setting and soon the area was reflecting brilliant oranges, pinks, and periwinkles.

"Come on," my father said, after a quick look around. "It's not good to be out here after dark."

We set up camp on the edge of the dead lake, my brothers building a large fire for us to sleep around. The nights here were cold. I sat on my mat nibbling on some smoked goat meat as I faced the dead lake.

I'd sprinkled a little salt on it, and I savored the smoky, chewy, salty combination. Salt is life. The moon had risen and it reflected off the lake, lighting up the night. A breeze blew and I wondered if there were ever witches out here and what would happen if I ran into one. I smiled. I knew what I'd do if there were.

I thought about the witch again. How I'd changed. How freeing my encounter with it was, especially after I'd chosen to run into it. I looked at my father, who'd always worked so hard. He'd allowed me to come along because I wanted to, but did he ever have the freedom I had?

"Papa," I said, "how . . . how did it happen? To your family?" The question was out of my mouth before I could stop it. I'd never asked Papa this. My brothers hadn't, either. I clapped my hands over my mouth, as if I could push the words back in and swallow them.

My father looked hard at me and both of my brothers sat up.

"Najeeba," Ger hissed. "Don't you ever think before speaking?"

I cringed, wanting to hide under my mat.

My father raised a hand. "No . . . I've been waiting

for one of you to ask." He paused. "I did not think it would be my daughter."

My brothers looked at each other. None of us knew what to do. My father, when angry, sometimes showed it in really complicated ways that were hard to read. It was best to just sit and take whatever it was.

CHAPTER 3

Arrows

This world is harsh, my children. Some who think they are so smart like to say that the Great Book is a toxic, even mystical tome that wrote the miserable fate of the Okeke into existence by force. I can understand these misguided people. To see such a great people brought so low, into this slavery, it's easy to imagine that something mystical is at work. But the Great Book is merely the messenger, a descriptor.

The first Osu-nu understood this, and that is what inspired them to step out. Adoro is a kind goddess. The marriage of our people to her freed us from the work and the resulting quick cruel death. That is part of why the other Okeke hate us. And even the Nuru had to respect what we did, though not without Adoro needing to show them her wrath when they did not, of course.

Eventually, however, the Nuru had to let us be, and to

this day, the Nuru mostly avoid the Osu-nu. This was two centuries ago. Now, we are the descendants of the ones who did something crazy, suicidal even, to be free of them. What is enduring Adoro's Cleanser to being a slave to the Nuru? It chooses only a few out of many. It is worth it.

We are outcasts from the enslaved; we are the Okeke whom the Okeke threw away. We are fine with that . . . mostly. Because we made our choice. We gave ourselves to Adoro, and Adoro protects us because we are hers. We live in freedom because of it. But this is not what I want to talk about today, children. Najeeba, you have finally asked for the story of my parents. I told myself I'd only tell the details of it if one of you asked.

You have asked, Najeeba.

Once these words are spoken, in many ways, they are written. You cannot swallow them back; you have to live with what comes next. Now you three will know. It is not a long or complicated tale, but it's a painful one. So listen closely, because I will never tell it to you again and there is no one else left who can tell it to you firsthand. I told your mother this story the night before we were married. If we were to wed, she deserved to know who I am fully. She was the first and only one I've told.

I grew up villages away from this one. My village was

called Adoro 19. My father and his brothers traveled the salt roads, too. They began taking me when I was ten years old. Early. I was tall and strong for my age and I took orders well. By the time I was thirteen, I was practically leading the caravan. I would get the call to leave before even my father. He was so proud of me. Our family was wealthy. My parents only had two children, my sister and me. We were twins.

My sister and I were close, though we did not spend a lot of time together. We had different sets of friends, but we both liked the same foods, had a habit of going to sleep at the same time, knew when the other was happy or sad. When I began going on the salt roads, we grew even more apart.

Then one year, the Adoro Cleanser came, and it took my sister. We were fifteen. I remember that day . . . I didn't know how to feel. The Cleanser is a mystery, and of all the young people in the village, it had chosen my sister. She was gone for three days. When she came back, she was never really the same. She was quieter and more secretive. She would do things and I'd only find out in some way that did not involve her telling me. That's not how we'd been before. And as if to balance things out, she grew more and more beautiful. Tall, slim, dark-skinned, with the face of a queen from a different time. I guess I also grew more into myself, but I didn't glow like her. When she spoke, which was rarely, everyone would listen. When she laughed, others felt good. But mostly she was quiet, and when I asked her about the Cleanser, she'd only frown and walk away.

When we were seventeen, my sister fell in love. I don't know how she met this boy. He was our age, but he was not Osu-nu. I remember that this made me nervous. She was so secretive, and her beauty was an additional juju, so deceiving him would be easy for her. She introduced me to him twice at the market, where tribe is ignored for the sake of commerce. It was immediately clear to me that this boy truly loved my sister and she loved him. I never got to ask how they met, though I wanted to know, to understand. Their love was like a glitch in a portable's ancient crumbling operating system. I didn't know what to think.

For the first time since the Cleanser had taken my sister, I saw her smile. She was still quiet and secretive, but she was so happy. She loved to cook and she'd whistle to herself while she cooked. My parents had begun to discuss finding her a husband. They didn't know about the boy, but now that she was happier, it seemed a good time to find her a spouse. She already had many strong prospects. The fact that she had been visited by the Cleanser had made her even more sought after.

The evening of the full moon, there were festivities in the village. Storytelling, singing, boys and girls went out and surfed the sand dunes with woven boards of raffia. Everyone was out and about. But . . . they still found us. Each. One by one. I was out on the dunes with my sister that evening. We'd spent days weaving our boards. She'd done a far better job on hers and so she flew past me down the dune. Some of our agemates were there, too. I was laughing and annoyed.

Something hit the sand right beside my sister. We were halfway down the giant dune. I glanced behind me. There was a group of people standing at the top of the sand dune. I turned back to my sister just in time to see her fly off her board and go tumbling. Something had hit her. My first thought was that birds were attacking her. Then a bird did attack her! A large bird. A hawk? An owl?! I couldn't tell in the moonlight. Something came at me and I managed to avoid it. I saw it pierce the sand just feet away as I zoomed past. A black arrow. At least it looked black.

I jumped off my board and ran to my sister. She was screaming and writhing as the bird slapped and clawed at her, shrieking and squawking. "Shada!" I shouted, beating at the bird. I grabbed its wings and yanked them back until I heard a crack. I threw it aside, where it continued to struggle. It had torn up her left arm. "Come on, Shada!

Get up!" I cried, glancing at the top of the sand dune. I pulled her up and she put an arm on my shoulder.

"Hurts," she gasped.

The people at the top of the dune were coming. There was a woman holding up a bow, an arrow nocked on it. We made it about ten steps before it felt like something kicked my sister. She screamed and went limp in my arms. An arrow protruded from her side. "Go, Manal! Go! Or they will kill you, too!" she groaned. Another arrow hit her in the neck and I turned and stared at them, furious. The woman was nocking another arrow.

"Osu-nu!!!!" someone called. "You defile our son? Deceitful whore! We will erase your bloodline. Adoro has already killed you."

I put my sister down. I fled for my life. Two arrows missed me, one that flew dangerously close to my head, another that hit the sand at my heels. My agemates were all running every which way. They reached nearby houses, jumped fences, hid in doorways, ran inside homes and buildings. I reached the village, ran down the road, ran behind houses. I was so pumped up on adrenaline and shock and horror . . . I just ran and ran. I didn't know if they were coming after me or not. Someone jumped from behind a building and tackled me. I kicked, fought, bit. I got away.

I hid in a doorway and one of them spotted me there, too. Again, I fought and then ran. And ran.

Finally, I made it to and hid in the Adoro temple outside the village.

My village's temple looks like the one back home near the Paper House, like any Adoro temple in any Osu-nu village. That red clay statue of the goddess stared at me with her penetrating gaze, as she grasped her staff with the skull on top. I threw myself into the pile of coal at her feet. And I could see myself do this in the huge dusty mirror behind her. If you are not Osu-nu, you'd have to have a death wish to go in there. I was out of my mind, so it wasn't a calculated action, but going into the temple was the smartest thing I could have done. I cowered in there all night, weeping and cursing. Seeing my sister's face.

I spoke terrible things into the world that night. Sacrilegious things. Praying that not only Adoro, but that Ani herself heard me. I'm ashamed to say that I meant every single word, every shout, every cry, with all my heart. When the sun returned, I went home. The air still smelled like smoke. I could hear people in homes still weeping. No one was outside. I fell to my knees when I got there. My home had been burned to the ground. The remains were still smoldering. A neighbor saw me. He rushed out and *pulled me into his home. He and his best friend told me what had happened.*

The family of the boy my sister loved and planned to marry found out she was Osu-nu. Humiliated, they set out to regain their honor. First they killed their own son, the boy my sister loved. They'd slit his throat and then set him aflame in front of their entire village. Then they'd come to our village and killed my sister, gone to my house and killed my parents, and then gone to my father's brothers' homes and killed both of them and their children in front of their families. They'd meant to kill me, but I'd gotten away.

My neighbor was going to market the next day and he took me with him, to get me out of the village. Once there, he gave me some money, hugged me, and wished me well—and suddenly, at the age of seventeen, I was on my own. I traveled far. I had died. I was no one. I was reborn. So I chose a new name. Xabief is the name of the boy my sister loved and who loved my sister. I have always been happiest when traveling the salt roads. That is one thing that has not changed.

My father finished talking, and in the firelight I could see his glistening cheeks. I had always known that something terrible had happened to my father's family. He held us all so closely and made sure we deeply understood our place in the world. My mother had told us we weren't allowed to ask him about it. I don't know what possessed me to ask this night. Maybe the sight of the dead lake had made me want to know the pained history of something. Sometimes I wondered if there was truly a place for love in this world of ours.

My father got up and walked away, toward the dead lake. We knew not to follow him. When the sun came up, he was back on his mat, fast asleep. We didn't speak any more of it after that. He never spoke of it again. Just as he'd promised.

CHAPTER 4

Alusi Juputalu Obodo Nine Di N'ani Ahia

[Spirits Fill All the Towns in the Land of the Market]

My father and brother Rayan went to the camel auction to buy my mother her new camel. My brother Ger and I waited for them in the salt seller's market. There were big sales happening all around us and it was irritating. No one's salt looked as good as what we'd mined. Especially that crystal-clear block my father had found. Plus, we were bored.

Unlike my brother, who did not have his face covered at all, I was wearing my weather-treated garments, my veil wrapped over my face. I felt bold and confident all covered up. No one could even tell I was a girl. I sashayed back and forth in front of our salt, my hands on my hips the way I'd seen Papa do when he spoke at village council meetings, making Ger laugh.

"Salt is life," I said, lowering my voice. "Look at me. I am a big man. Full of salt!" My brother was practically crying with laughter now.

"Bring your wife's soup here. I will make it salty!" I looked around. The market was mesmerizing. Men and boys walking up and down, stopping to listen to sellers talk about their salt and how great it was. All these Osu-nu men and boys had been to the dead lake at different places and different times, never crossing paths. And they came here to sell what they had gathered. They didn't look like the non-Osu-nu Okeke who came to buy from them, the most obvious difference being that the Osu-nu sellers looked dusty and travel-worn. This market was not far from Okeke villages and towns. Most had not had to travel as far as we Osu-nu had come.

I was a girl, yet I'd traveled the salt roads, too. I'd seen the magnificent dead lake. I had personally chopped free some of the salt we had on display. My salt would be sold. I was a part of all this, too. The aura of the travel was on me, as was my encounter with the witch . . . I felt bold and unique. I suddenly had a crazy idea.

"Ger," I said. "Watch this!" I jumped on top of one of our salt cubes. "Everyone, whatever you are look-ing at is nonsense. See the finest salt right here at Xabief Enterprises! Like cubes of frozen water. Like a capture station malfunctioned. Come see for yourself. No sand, no dirt, no preserved creatures. Pure pure pure salt that will wash annnnny impurity from the body."

"Ah ah, Jeeba, what are you doing?" I heard Ger hiss. He tried to grab my arm, but I snatched it away and kept talking. It was like stepping out of myself a bit. It was like singing. It felt natural, easy, right. And it was exciting. No one could see that I was a girl, be-cause I was all covered up. I was tall and lean; it wasn't hard for me to fool them. I had lowered my voice a bit. Plus, girls did not attend the salt markets, let alone make sales. So I had assumption on my side, as well.

I looked grown men right in the eye, glad that Mama wasn't here to see me behaving so badly. The men around us were soon surrounding Ger and me, demanding to see our salt, shaking sacks of coin. I knew Ger wouldn't do anything. If people here knew I was a girl, they might run us out of the market, or probably worse. He moved back and said nothing. I just kept talking and talking. If I stopped, I was sure I'd lose control of the situation. And I was enjoying myself. Within that hour, I negotiated and sold *all* of our salt. I even sold the super clear cube my father had found for an amount so high, Ger had kicked me and whispered, "Do not mess this up. Papa will be so angry if you do."

When people finally moved on since we had nothing more to sell, only then did I process what I had done.

"You are too reckless!" Ger hissed at me. He pulled me close to him. "I could slap you right now! You could be *killed* for what you've done!"

Now that whatever had come over me had left, I just felt tired and terrified. The mantra of, "What have I done, what have I done, what have I done?!" repeated in my head. I'd always had a spontaneous side. I'd blurt things at my teachers, I'd once slapped an age-mate, I'd thrown a rock at the meanest village cat, I would eat the rest of the dates even though I knew my father wanted to eat them, I had run into the witch and been taken by it. I wouldn't think things through, I'd just act. My brothers knew this about me. But I had never, ever done anything this extreme.

"I don't know what got into me," I said. "Ger . . . tell Papa *you* did it." I shoved one of the sacks of coin at him. There was a huge pile of them surrounding us. We didn't even know how to store them, the chests we'd brought all filled up.

Ger looked at me like I had lost my mind. He did not take the sack. "How can I do that? *You* did it."

"I'm a girl!" I whispered. I looked around.

"A stupid one."

I shoved the sack toward him some more. "Please, brother!"

Ger stared hard at me, then his face softened. "Fine."

I sighed, relieved, as he snatched the sack from me. We both looked around. No one was paying attention to us anymore.

"Go and prepare the camels," he said. "And keep your veil on."

"Of course," I said.

"And shut up. No more talking."

———

Papa and Rayan returned from the camel auction with a young white camel that my father had already named Noor. She had strange blue eyes, and my father had gotten a good deal on her because she was somewhat small, despite being full-grown. "Your mother will like this one," my father said. He froze, staring at us. "Where is all our—"

My brother spoke quickly and I moved to look at Noor. I needed to hide the fact that I was shaking. I wanted to sit down. I petted the new camel instead. Her fur was rough but very healthy. My father had gotten a good deal. I looked into her blue eyes, trying to block out all that my brother was saying. I could see Rayan watching me, though.

My father was so stunned that he did what I'd wanted to do, sat right there on the ground. "You sold *all* the salt. All of it. In one day. This is what we will rely on for the year. We cannot go again until next year, o. That is the way. This is our livelihood and you risked it all pretending to be what you are not. Why?"

"I . . . I don't know."

I tensed up, holding eye contact with Noor.

"Papa, I was not trying to be you," Ger continued. "You built this business, not me. It is your legacy. We . . . I just saw an opportunity."

Our father only sighed, looking miserable.

"How could you let this happen?" Rayan snapped at me.

I opened my mouth to speak and quickly shut it

as Ger went and stood at the sacks of money. Rayan's attention went from me to the sacks. The sacks were not small. My father stared at them, nudging them with his foot. He looked at Ger, frowning, fully understanding now.

Rayan reached for a sack and lifted it to his face. He gasped when he felt the heft. "How much did you . . ." He looked around at the salt market. Everyone was too busy haggling to pay attention to us. For now.

We bought some supplies for the journey home. Then we left quickly.

My father had never seen so much money at one time in his life. He'd never heard of such a thing. We'd made seven times what we normally made. The cube he'd found had brought in such a windfall that, technically, the business would be fine if we didn't return for another two years!

"What did you do?" my father asked Ger, the market in the distance.

He was riding beside my father with Rayan. I was behind them leading Noor. I was glad Ger couldn't look at me.

"I . . . I . . ." he chuckled. "I just sang to them. We

were bored and I stood up and just started talking camelshit. Well, not camelshit. The truth, really. But with style, panache . . . and people listened and then they saw. Wouldn't have worked without having the actual product."

"You will do it again next year," my father said. "I will leave. Maybe that was why they gave you a chance."

Now Ger did look back at me. "Only if Najeeba comes," Ger said. "She . . . might have been part of the chemistry, too."

"Me?" I said, shocked.

Rayan scoffed. "She shouldn't have been there in the first place. It's men's work."

This annoyed me, and I found myself arguing against my better judgment . . . again. "I *knew* when we should leave," I insisted. "I belonged as much as—"

"No, you don't," Rayan said.

I felt like exploding.

"There is nothing written that says a girl cannot be present at the salt market," my father said with a wave of his hand. "It's just a culture norm. Anyway, Ger, I'm proud of you. I didn't know you had it in you."

"I didn't either," he said. "Thank you, Papa."

I could almost hear Rayan's glower. *Let him broil*, I

thought. He was the oldest, the most entitled. My father's successor, so I understood his irritation. But my father's business was the family's business, as it would be for whichever of us came after my father. Hierarchy was irrelevant in the grand scheme of things. When the business benefited, we all benefited. At the same time, what in Ani had I just allowed Ger to rope me into? Also at the same time, a part of me was excited by the prospect. What I'd done was wrong, but I loved it.

━━━

When Papa told Mama how much we'd made, I could hear her scream of surprise and joy through Papa's portable. Then she immediately asked, "Who knows about this? Did you make sure you weren't followed?"

"We left the market quickly," Papa assured her.

The salt markets were fairly safe, but the amount we'd made could turn honest men into thieves and murderers very quickly. Leaving early was smart, but what also helped us was the intense storm that hit the area about an hour after we left. We could see it in the distance as we traveled. Papa shouted to the sky, "Ani is magnificent!" over and over. Then, for the rest of the journey home, we had to endure him playing and forcing us to recite the Great Book.

———

When we finally reached our village, a small parade greeted us. Almost all of Mama's many friends, several of the village elders and officials, the village reporter using her portable to take notes, a group of dancers who threw senti leaves at us, and many laughing children. Mama had arranged for it. And it wasn't difficult for her to do, because once she told people of the village about what had happened, it was a natural move. Every salt gatherer gave a certain percentage of his earnings to the village, so our windfall was a windfall for everyone.

Two small masquerades made of packed dried raffia and draped with red cloth stood at the town line, and they greeted us in the old language of Igbo. One of their voices was female, and I was sure that I recognized it—it was that of my math teacher, Kam. I was certain that the other was the overseer from the Paper House.

"Welcome, salt gatherers," they both said as we passed. "You are our pride! You are our joy! The village thrives because of you. We are happy your journey was fruitful and safe. Xabief, you are a true father! Rayan and Ger, you have great footsteps to fill, but you are already on your way!" They did not call out my name.

Needless to say, this journey had changed me. Profoundly. Since running into it, I had dreams about the witch every night. The sight of the dead lake had filled me with pride for my people, who were the only ones who could see it. I now knew why my father was the way he was. What I had done at the market made me feel powerful and taught me that, even as a thirteen-year-old girl, I could walk tall amongst men. And the journey back home had been beautiful and peaceful— with a hint of fear, because for all those days, we were never sure if we would be ambushed for the fortune we carried. My father had given me my own shift to guard the camp, and I'd learned what it was to watch and sit with the desert night. I was so much more than the girl I'd been when I left home.

But their omission of my name, even with all my growth, made me take it all and pack it tightly. It shrank me. Made me small again, despite my size. And quiet. As we rode into town, surrounded by laughing, joyful, proud neighbors, family, friends, I saw Peter and

Obi amongst the faces. I wanted to hide. No one threw fragrant dried senti leaves at me. No one rushed forward to hand me bottles of olive oil and honey. It was as if people didn't really see me. Honestly, I wasn't sure I wanted them to, since what I'd done could get me killed. Better to be invisible . . . but being invisible is just unpleasant. No one wants to be invisible. They crowded my father and brothers, but I was alone, watching it all happen from behind, as I rode beside Noor.

The moment we reached home, I hopped off Abdul and ran inside, even before I could hug my mother. And my mother, who was laughing and hugging my father and shouting songs with the women around her, didn't notice me, anyway. There were people surrounding our home, and it became a small celebration. However, I hid inside, crying. To grow so much and then contract, to step onto your path, even when you didn't quite know it was a path, and then to suddenly shrink yourself . . . it hurt. And to do something amazing . . . that could get you killed . . . none of it felt good. I couldn't really articulate it, though. I was too young and it was all so complex. But I *felt* it.

I locked my bedroom door, shut my window,

and lay on my bed and sobbed and sobbed. The muffled sound of celebration music outside was a sad
soundtrack to my pain. At some point, there came a
tapping at my window. I froze, listening and trying to
will whoever it was to go away forever. When the tapping persisted, I got up.

"Leave me alone," I said. "I'm . . . tired!"

"Liar! Open up."

I paused. Then I smiled and opened the window.
It was Peter. Obi was with her, too. As they climbed in,
I could see a bit of the celebration happening outside.
People were dancing and the air smelled of roasted
meat. I shut the window as soon as they were both in.
Peter was wearing a bright yellow dress and no shoes,
her feet dusty from dancing in the sand. She looked
me up and down. "Have you gotten even taller?" she
asked.

I rolled my eyes and sat on my bed. "No," I said.

Obi, who was dressed in a long, dark blue caftan
and pants, leaned against the closed window and
looked very hard at me. "How was it?"

"Amazing," I said. I told them much, but I didn't
tell them about the witch or what I'd done at the market. It was all still quite a story, and the fact that I had

survived and, in many ways, flourished, changed the way they viewed me. The effect of my experience on me wasn't that obvious yet, though.

They stayed with me most of the night while the celebration outside raged. They told me about how word had spread amongst our peers about me going and it had caused a lot of fights between boys and girls, parents and daughters. I had started a conversation that no one knew they needed to have.

CHAPTER 5

The Paper House

I met Peter at the Paper House wearing my long white flowing dress. There was a strong breeze and I worried that my garments would get dirty. I was about fourteen at this time, not long before my second trip on the salt roads.

"What took you so long?" Peter said.

"I came as quickly as I could. I don't live as close as you."

The front and back doors to the Paper House were a deep, vibrant blue. You could see them from afar, even at dusk. And they did not fade in the harsh sunlight. Blue doors keep spirits, ghosts, and gods out, at least according to the Paper House overseer. I didn't think a beautiful door would keep any of those out; if anything, it was an invitation to come in. Especially considering what was inside.

The large double doors were made of thick, braided

wrought-iron bars inscribed with a dead alphabet known as "bassa vah." The overseer said there was a manuscript that translated bassa vah into Okeke, but I'd never bothered to read it. That was more Peter's interest. She liked to know what everything meant.

You grasped the door handle, which was always warm from the sun, even at night, then you pushed. The door didn't open unless you gave it some energy, but once you got it moving, it did the rest. And then came the blast of cool air. Not from a capture station, but from an old machine made specially for cooling the air. It was the only one in our village, though I had heard that there were plenty in the horrific Seven Rivers Kingdom. Mixed with the cool air was the disinfectant mist that came from sprayers on the left and right. Our clothes, skin, hair, and sandals were officially free of anything that had decided to piggyback into the Paper House.

We stepped beyond the misters, and the smell came next—the musky sweet scent of distant vanilla, wood, dust, earth, coffee, smoke, and perfumed oil. It emanated from the thousands of ancient manuscripts, papers, and books. I wasn't a big reader like Peter, but the smell was like the past and the future. It always made me feel like I was in the right place.

The Paper House was a large, one-story house with blue walls and rows and rows and aisles and aisles and stacks and stacks. At the center were fifteen heavy wooden desks; this was where girls and women from all over the village sat and read. The overseer knew where everything was, but the overseer was not a nice man and he didn't like to be bothered. Wherever he was, he was always reshelving, reading, and documenting. Plus, a new load of manuscripts had come in, and he had been spending most of his time poring over them. So you had to pick and choose when to ask him questions.

"I'm going to ask the overseer about the new haul," Peter said with a grin. "I've been waiting patiently to give him time. Today is definitely the day." She was always so excited whenever we came into this place. The fact that she was here practically every day didn't matter.

I smiled. "You're brave to bother an archivist who's just gotten new things to archive, but all right." Perfect. This was not a book or manuscript search that I wanted company on, and I hadn't been sure how to tell Peter that I wanted to be alone. She was always so curious about everything, and she'd have forced me to tell her what I was looking for. "I'll be around," I said.

Peter dashed off through the arrangements of desks occupied by quiet girls and women reading books and papers. I went to the left into the stacks. I had an idea where to look.

I'd been working my way slowly through a section of crumbling manuscripts that all seemed to be about meditation and good health. I'd learned various exercises and stretches that I'd tried a few times. I preferred to read about things that I could do rather than stories that made me imagine. Imagining always made me feel uncomfortable. But writings that taught me how to physically do something, especially rest or relax, were more my speed. These manuscripts often veered toward the mystical in weird ways. There were torn pages from books, fully intact books, rigid pages handwritten in the most perfect writing I'd ever seen. Some written by hand, some by computer, all from a very different time.

Everything was somehow in order. The overseer was truly a master archivist. I don't know how he did it; it was probably why he was so mean. There was a sorcery section. It was small, with only stiff pages that smelled like incense. I stepped up to this stack. Some were in Okeke, some in Nuru, Sipo, most were in languages I could not understand. There was a piece of dirty paper that claimed to document the movements and logic of the Cleanser. I quickly skipped over that one. There was always going to be some nonsense in the treasure. I dragged over the stone stool beside a different aisle and sat on it in front of the stack. I sighed.

"What am I even *looking* for?" I muttered. "I don't know." I thought about what had happened last year when the witch took me up. When it seemed I'd come out of my body and into another. "A beginning," I muttered as I began to rifle through the papers. I could speak a little basic Nuru, and I could read it far better than I could speak it. My mother had taught me. "You don't need to speak to them, for they will never speak to you, only at you," she had told me years ago. "But someday, you will need to understand what you are dealing with."

I didn't know if that was true, but when I pulled up the circular piece of stiff paper written in Nuru, I could read the essay about medicine men who spent their entire lives trying to die. The writing did not read left to right, but in a counter-clockwise spiral that started on the outside and went around and around until it ended in the center. Tiny, neat, dense, frantic writing. It was all about trying to leave one's body behind. My belly fluttered as I took the piece of paper and stood up. I looked toward the reading tables. Peter would be there and she would ask me what I was reading. I sat back down on the stool and leaned against a stack of books.

There I read.

It was an account written by a woman who was one of those who'd spent her life trying to die. She'd starved herself, prayed, run into the desert until she lost all her water and was burned by the sun, all kinds of things. The woman called herself Mumtaz and she wrote as if she'd bled each sentence.

I don't remember the sun going down. I don't remember crying. And I don't remember the overseer walking up to me. All I know is that when I looked up, my face wet with tears, there he was in his brilliant white agbada like the grandchild of Ani, and the windows above were not the brilliant blue of the day sky, but the dark of the evening. "Stop reading that," he said, frowning. "It's dangerous."

I blinked. My eyes were so dry.

"You're reading *The Laws of the Earth*. That whole

manuscript was considered deified medicine to people back then."

"What does that even mean?" I asked. My mouth felt so dry.

"It means that you're in over your head," he said, taking the manuscript from me. "I'm sure you've read enough to satisfy your curiosity."

I nodded. I had.

"Are you well enough to go home?"

"Yes," I said. But I wasn't sure. I still felt light-headed. Dehydrated.

"You're Xabief's daughter, right?"

"I am."

"Of course you would find the most dangerous manuscript in the Paper House," he said. "You are the only girl of Adoro 5 to travel the salt roads of men." He laughed to himself. "I'll have to keep an eye on you."

"Yes, oga," I said, standing up.

He turned to leave and then turned back, an inquisitive look on his face. "What is it like?" he asked. "The dead lake, the roads. I . . . I was apprenticed early to archive and have never been."

I grinned. "It's another world."

He looked down his nose at me. Then after sev-

eral moments, he said, "There are more worlds in these."
He motioned around him. "The places in these books
and on this paper are somewhere."

"Maybe," I muttered. But I didn't really agree. There
was nothing like seeing the dead lake with your own
eyes, touching the salt with your hands, finding and
excavating cubes of it. He helped me up and I slowly
walked away from him down the corridor of stacked
books and manuscripts.

"Girl," he said behind me.

I turned around.

"Ani has blessed you. But don't come looking for
this manuscript again."

"I won't, overseer."

I walked past the desks. Only two women sat reading. Neither of them was Peter. Maybe she'd thought
I'd gone home without her. She'd be annoyed with
me, then. The moment I left the Paper House, the heat
of the evening blew over me like another world. I
stood there for a moment. What time was it? It felt
late. Maybe past nine p.m. Still, I took my time walking home.

What had the overseer meant by "The Laws of the
Earth" and "deified medicine"? And I couldn't look
any of it up now. The overseer would be watching me.

I considered sneaking back in later that night. The Paper House did not close, and though the overseer lived in the Paper House, he had to sleep at some point. I stopped and looked back at the Paper House. I turned and kept walking. *No,* I thought. *I know what I read. Definitions and reading about things in books is not what I need.* I needed to practice.

I went home and found that my father was not back yet and my mother was holding a meeting of the local council in the main room. I hadn't been missed. Well, unless you count my mother's white, blue-eyed camel, Noor, who'd trotted up to me from her stable. Noor was easily the friendliest camel I'd ever met. Not even my camel Abdul, whom I'd known for six years, greeted me like Noor. I patted Noor on the throat and smacked her rump. "Go back, Noor. I'll bring you salt to lick later," I said, and she did. I peeked inside, and my mother saw and nodded at me. Then she went back to talking to the ten or so elected village officials gathered. I went to my garden and sat amongst the yams.

Mumtaz, I thought. She'd written about what it was to leave the body. She'd called it "traveling." How can one spend an entire life trying to die? *You said if you are capable of traveling, you will first have a clear, memorable, and strange sign. It will be unexpected and in many ways make little sense. And once you have this sign, you will have a marker that you can always go back to.* I looked at the sky. "The witch," I muttered.

Mumtaz had then rambled on about her "marker," the place where she could grow most still, which was the center of the market when it was busiest. She'd stand there and people would walk around her, buying, selling, laughing, rushing, thinking, talking, bartering, watching. She'd tune into this. She'd grow still, as everything around her moved about. Then she'd just . . . travel.

At first, she'd thought she was finally dying. But it wasn't death. She was leaving. She rambled on about how traveling felt, growing more and more frantic. "I could see the market below," she wrote. "I was standing there. Just *standing there*! I looked like someone lost. I'd lost my soul. No one noticed me. Oh Allah, you could not have known such a thing until you did it, until it happened. And I felt . . . I could *feel*. I was light. My body has always felt so heavy. I cannot run fast or jump high. I am like a creature made of lead. But like this, when I traveled, I was a piece of wind. The freedom of it, the joy of it!"

Then she started writing about all that she saw and for some reason, I couldn't remember any of the details. I took a deep breath and imagined that place in front of the sand dune. The witch. The heat in the air. The smell of dust. The sting of sand, even from where my Papa and I were on our camels. The feeling of jumping off my camel and the rush in my veins when I started running and realized what I was about to do. Without a thought. Without a care for my safety. Deaf to my father's cries for me to stop. The sound of my sandals on the sand as I ran. The witch whirling before me with power and speed. The sound of it. The sting of its sand. My feet lifting off the ground.

I gasped. My chest arched forward and my head whipped back. Then my shoulders curled and my head whipped forward. "Ugh," I grunted. I flew forward. Through the yams, then the tomatoes, then I was tumbling. I must have gone through the fence. *How?* I thought. I was rolling into the dirt road. And yet I was still going. I made it to the neighbor's yard. They grew nothing but prickly pear cactuses. I tumbled through them. I didn't feel the sting of their tiny thorns. I was slowing down. Finally, I stopped right in front of the fat black cat who loved to sleep amongst the cactuses.

The cat opened his eyes and stared lazily at me as I tried to get up. I couldn't get up. I gasped as I tried and tried. It was dark and I couldn't see myself at all.

I was rolling on the ground, in the dust. "What is . . ." My voice! It felt like my throat was full of ash, and I sounded like I was a thousand miles away. From myself! "I can't . . . what is happening?!" The cat's ears turned toward me, and he clearly saw me, getting up and stretching his body and shaking out his furry coat. He strolled toward me, unbothered by my struggle. Then he sat and stared at me.

"Hey," I whispered in my strange voice. Dust blew toward the cat as if my voice were a breeze. The cat snuffled and twitched back. He sauntered off, his tail high in the air, showing his furry white balls. I tried rolling over and found that I could not. *Okay*, I thought. *Calm down.* It was too dark for me to see myself, but as I relaxed, I began to understand something profound—I was *not* in my body. *I am something else*, I thought. I felt myself on the verge of total panic and I fought to hold on to my logical self. *If I am not myself, then I cannot move as if I am*, I thought. I must have lain there for minutes as I tried to figure things out.

Then, from afar, I heard my mother calling my name. "Najeeba! What is wrong with you?" Panic. But the sound of her voice made something deep in me heat up. "Najeeba!" Her voice was more frantic now and the heat within me increased. I heard the voices of others, some also calling my name, and then I was flying. Back the way I'd come. Through the prickly pears. Tumbling across the road, like some kind of desert plant caught in the wind. Back into the garden. Into my body.

My mother was shaking me, her hands on my shoulders, her nails digging into my flesh, her assistant on one side of me and one of the town's council leaders on the other. My body whipped back again, knocking my mother from me. Her assistant shrieked, jumping up, and the council leader gasped and ran off, holding his chest. Dust and dirt burst from below me, and soon everyone was coughing, including me. My mother was back on her feet, looking down at me, her eyes wide. Now her assistant ran off.

"What . . ."

"I don't know, Mama," I gasped, still on the ground.

"Are you all right?" my mother asked after another moment.

"I . . ." My mother raised a hand and I stopped talking. She turned and left. Then she returned with a glass of water. Just as I had not spoken of it with my father, my mother and I didn't speak of it now. I never spoke of any of it with my parents. Maybe I wasn't supposed to. I'd never know, because I had no point of context. I didn't speak of it with Peter, nor Obi. I was too afraid to speak to the overseer. I had no books or manuscripts I could use to mine information. I had no mentor or elder who could impart knowledge on me. This thing was mine and mine alone.

Eventually, I started leaving my body often. But never at home. Only while out in the desert. I had vivid dreams where I was a giant beautiful serpent creature who smelled like smoke, olive oil, and honey and flew over all the lands. The dreams would scare me and I would run to my mother, who would think priming me with flatbread and juicy dates was enough to get me to forget about the dreams. I'd then go to my father and he'd tell me to embrace the dreams and that they were a good omen.

CHAPTER 6

Constantly Shifting Sands

I went with my father and brothers again on the salt roads. I knew when it was time to leave, but this time, I didn't say anything. I wasn't sure if I wanted to go. I'd had a year of everyone treating me differently, some better, some worse. Younger kids began to look to me for advice. One of my agemates who'd been taken and returned by the Cleanser didn't even get the respect I got. Obi began treating me more like a male friend than a female one. Peter was engaged to be married and hadn't invited me to her women's circle for the announcement. And I'd recently discovered that I could leave my body and had been privately honing this skill whenever I could.

So much changed in that year. And so when I woke up about thirteen months after the journey and I knew it was time to go again, I said nothing. But my brother Ger did. He insisted that I go, citing how helpful I'd been last year. My father and, surprisingly, my brother Rayan agreed. As did my mother. They all expected me to be excited. I was. I was for the same reason Ger had insisted I go.

But there was one other reason that only I knew. And on our way to the dead lake, on those days when we camped early and I had time to myself, I went for walks alone. And once or twice, I snuck off when everyone was asleep. Finally, I could truly be alone and relaxed enough to really . . . travel.

In the silence and loneliness of the vast desert, I'd sit on the sand and I'd remember Mumtaz's words. Then I'd think my own words, centering my mind and self, imagining the witch in all her dust and wind and how she took me . . . and I'd leave. I'd look down at myself. It was a strange sight. Whereas before it had looked like I was asleep, the more I did it, the more I began to simply look like I was staring off into space. I then turned and just flew. In this way, I learned what the salt roads looked like from high above. You could see the trail in the desert, even over the sand dunes. As if the salt roads had always been there, or, more likely, were there by mystical means, for how else could a trail remain with the constantly shifting sands?

I went flying like this when we reached the dead lake, too, telling Papa and my brothers that I was going for a walk. In that hour alone, amongst the salt cubes and shards much closer to them than they knew, I sat on the hard smooth surface of a large cube that was dusky with detritus. It was warm from the shining sun. I centered myself and, after minutes of staring across the crystalline world, imagining the witch dancing and dislodging the biggest shards, sending them high into the air, I felt myself begin to rise from my body. I looked down. I had a smile on my face. I urged myself to bring my fist up and cough into it as I floated higher and higher. I saw myself do so. "Okay," I said, my voice sounding like the wind. "That is a new discovery."

I wondered if I could make my body do other things while I was away. But how could I know when I was not there? I flew higher over the dead lake. Time and space were different when I flew; this time I flew fast and very very far. So far that I began to see the end of the salt and the beginning of another land. There were patches of what might have been dry scrub grass between the salt shards. I worried about my physical body, so I turned around and went back. But I'd learned something else—there was an end to the dead lake. And beyond it was something more. When I reentered my body, I shivered and whispered, "Possibilities." My mouth was so dry and I felt so cold. The salt I sat on was still warm, so I stayed there for a few more minutes. According to my portable, I'd been gone for twenty minutes.

"Possibilities," I muttered again as I stood up and stretched my legs. As I looked at the dead lake, it already seemed different to me. I'd seen its end. I could contain it in my mind now.

When I returned to Papa and my brothers, they greeted me, but that was it. They couldn't see or sense any change in me. I was glad. I liked my secret being mine.

When we arrived at the market, I was nervous. I kept looking at Ger, but he wouldn't look at me. Was I really going to do this again? Would he stay quiet about it? So many men and boys doing what only men and boys were supposed to do. There was a lot of shouting, posturing, sizing up. And there wasn't a girl or woman in sight. Though I knew it as a fact, I hadn't been so aware of this last year. I'd spent weeks with my father and brothers, so being around more men and boys hadn't seemed like anything to me, even if I wasn't supposed to be there. I hadn't planned to do anything last year until I'd done it. This year was different.

I wore my veil and no one paid me any mind. Eventually, as my father and Rayan focused all their attention toward prepping Ger, I relaxed some.

"You ready, son?" my father said to him. "You loose and relaxed?"

"I'm . . . a little nervous, but it'll be all right," he said.

Rayan patted him on the back as he looked around. "It's going to be more than all right."

Then he raised his voice. "Xabief Enterprises has the finest salt in the market."

A few men turned toward us upon hearing the name. They remembered us. I felt a tingle of excitement. My nerves weren't settling, but they didn't feel so terrible anymore. "You're going to leave, right?" Ger said. "Both of you."

"You don't want us here?" Papa asked.

"Like last time," Ger said. He smiled a shaky smile. "So I can do my thing. No pressure."

He wiggled his arms. "Loose and relaxed."

This pleased Papa, who nodded. "Okay. We'll be back in an hour to see how you're doing. Jeeb, come get us if there's any problem."

"I will," I said. The excitement had traveled all over my body now and I felt out of breath. Thankfully, neither Papa nor Rayan noticed me, so focused they were on Ger. I watched them go, feeling tense and a little dizzy. I looked at the salt we had to sell. My father's knack had proven itself yet again—he'd found another treasure. This time on his last search. We'd found a lot of good cubes, but nothing truly stunning, and Papa had begun to grow annoyed with himself. He was always able to find something, and usually it didn't take this long. He'd been gone for two hours when he returned with it. The salt cube was about the size of his hand, but it was perfectly clear with a hint of pink. Such cubes were highly sought after because of their taste.

"Najeeba," Ger said when my father and brother were gone.

"I'm scared."

"No, you're not," he said.

I wasn't.

"Don't take off your veil."

"I know."

He pushed me toward the stool, whispering, "Just do what you did last time. And you *cannot* get caught."

I looked at the stool, feeling a rush of adrenaline.

My hands shook. I didn't really know how I'd done it. I blinked and it crept into me like hot wind. I could. I could do it.

"Do it," I heard Ger say. "I see you. You can."

I was taller than I had been last year, and the second time you do something extraordinary is rarely as difficult as the first if you have the talent, which I did. Even more so now.

I stepped onto the stool and loudly sang, "Who is the one who will walk away from here with the finest salt of Xabief Enterprises? Whose daughter will attract the best husband? Whose wife will be most pleased? Whose meals will be most delicious? Who will not see even the smallest illness? Come on. Let's find out!" The men of the salt market quickly gathered and I'd never felt so powerful.

At first I just sang to them. Collected them to me. Then I don't quite recall how it went. Not in a way that I could explain to you. At some point, it was like the witch blew into the market and swept me up and left me behind at the same time. My brother Ger said it was like I was possessed.

I was loud, poised, poetic, and he said I looked like I was having the time of my life. He didn't have to do anything but help men load salt onto carts. I sold the special salt cube to a Nuru man who looked like someone very important. He'd come to us with an entourage of what looked like five soldiers and he'd told them to stay where they were as he approached me. All this Ger told me. We were surrounded by quite a crowd of mostly Okeke, but a few were Nuru, and all of them stepped back to let the man come to me. He'd spoken directly to me and I had looked him right in the eye the entire time.

"Like you were equals," Ger said afterward. He leaned toward me and whispered this, but he didn't look around. He was no longer as afraid or disturbed by my actions. "And you *squeezed* him! You spoke circles around him without insulting him. I think he could have had us arrested or even killed. But you just walked this balance and you *squeezed* him to pay up. In front of everyone. Who would believe this?!" He clapped me hard on the back and laughed.

For the second year in a row, I sold all the salt we had mined. Our last customers had just positioned the final cubes of salt onto their cart. They slowly pushed the cart away and there stood Papa, Rayan beside him. Both glared at me. They'd been in the audience the entire time. They'd watched me do what I was so good at doing; they'd watch Ger allow it. I glanced at Ger; he looked mortified.

"Papa," I whispered. "I—"

"Pack up," he snapped. *"Now."*

We packed up, loading the sacks of money into the chests; we'd brought more of them this time.

"What in Ani's name did you think you were doing?" Rayan whispered to me as I made to get on Abdul.

"Shhh!" our father hissed. "No talking. Move. Quickly."

I could barely tighten Abdul's straps. I was dizzy with fear and shock. I couldn't imagine what my father thought. Ger and I had lied. I was a girl in a salt market selling salt for the highest price the market had probably ever seen. The name Xabief Enterprises was known now, especially after this second year in a row of big sales. If anyone found me out, Okeke or Nuru, my being Osu-nu, they'd probably kill me. I'd outsmarted and therefore humiliated so many.

We were out of the market even faster than last year, buying the bare minimum of supplies, and in the vastness of the desert within an hour. As we moved, Rayan kept looking back. We were able to move quickly because we'd bought almost nothing at the market and our supplies were still tightly bundled. All we had were our camels and the sacks of money, which, plenty as it was, was much lighter and smaller than the salt. We made good time.

"Was it you last year?" Papa asked, breaking two hours of silence. I was riding beside Ger, Rayan behind us. Ger and I looked at each other. I couldn't read Ger's face.

"Yes," I said.

"*Kai!!*" Papa shouted. "My daughter. *This* is my daughter!"

"Where did you learn to do that?" Rayan asked, his camel moving up to trot beside me.

"I . . . I don't know. Something just . . . I didn't learn."

Papa began to pray loudly. Then he turned to me. "I enjoy having you here, Jeeb. Don't you like being out here with me, with us?"

"Yes, Papa," I insisted. "I love it. It feels like . . . I belong out here with you. Even if I am a girl."

Papa nodded. "Do you see how we all said you should come this second time?"

Rayan nodded.

Ger said nothing.

"We know how people back home behaved last year, ignoring you. It is understandable. But we are the ones who were with you. We know you belong here."

"I do," I said. "I didn't say it, but I had the call again this time. I knew wh—"

"Then why would you *do* this?"

I said nothing.

"You have put us all in danger," Rayan said. "People may come after us tonight. Do you know who that Nuru man was? That is the one they call The Haboob, one of the wealthiest Nuru merchants in Seven·Rivers! If he learns that he just haggled with a fourteen-year-old Osu-nu *girl*, he'll have you bought, sold, raped, and killed, and maybe not even in that order! Then he'll do the same to Mama! Then us!"

I whimpered.

"You provided him with something of incredible quality," Papa said. "He can't argue that you cheated him. That will make him even angrier!"

We were all quiet for a while. I couldn't help looking behind us, now. There was no one.

But the sky was clear, too. No storm to hold back anyone who wanted to come after us.

"That witch taught you," Papa muttered. "I should have known there would be a consequence. Now its alusi lives in you. There is always a price."

"Witch?" Ger asked.

Papa only shook his head. "We have to focus on making it home alive."

We made it home alive. And we had made twice as much money as the year before. My father didn't tell my mother until we got home, and therefore there was no celebration. Our return home was quiet. But our village was once again replenished by our profit. Word got around about what we'd done, but the mystics of one caravan on each salt road at a time and rigid Osu-nu law kept other caravans from following us. No one group ever got the call at the same time. And here we were doing it again. Other men must have wondered what Papa's secret was, but how could they ever find it out?

We rebuilt the old parts of our home and expanded on some of it, building a lavish and spacious main room for the family. This room also became a place for community meetings, ceremonies, celebrations, and a place where my agemates came to study for school. Adoro 5 flourished, with enough money to maintain the dirt roads, the schools, and even the Paper House. Peter and Obi were now used to me going, and Obi had also gone on his first journey. Peter's marriage was finally set for next year.

When another year rolled by, when I was fifteen, I woke up knowing it was time to go again. I was excited, unsure, and a little sad. And there was Papa standing at my door, looking at me. I couldn't see his face because sunlight was shining in behind him. I sat up.

A week later, I accompanied my father and brothers on the salt roads. And at the market, I made my family and community even more money with my strange gift.

CHAPTER 7

Salt Water and Ghosts

By the time I was sixteen, a good third of the girls in my village were joining their fathers on the salt roads journey. Word had spread about my brother Ger's success with selling my father's salt at the market, and several in the village said that my presence was what gave him the confidence to do what he did. So girls began to be sent on the salt roads for good luck and prosperity. In a matter of three years, my actions had changed the way my entire village had done things for decades. I was learning a lot about myself and it was growing my sense of power and worth in a quiet way, but knowing that being myself could make such a profound change in such a short period of time taught me a deeper lesson.

Only Papa and my brothers knew I was the one doing the bargaining. We didn't tell Mama. If she had known, she'd never have allowed it. Unlike for Papa and my brothers, her fear for my safety would have outweighed the promise of money and the freedom of letting me use my gift.

I told no one about my traveling, my flying. Not even Peter and Obi. Who would understand it, really? Maybe the overseer. He might have even suspected something after catching me reading those papers years ago. He'd watched me closely ever since, whenever I went to the Paper House, which was less and less as I got older. He often suggested books and manuscripts to me whenever I went there, and they were always about desert life, plant life, connecting to nature.

I enjoyed reading them, but maybe there was something he wanted me to find in those books too, for there is a thin line between the natural and the mystical. He once told me this as he handed a manuscript to me about how to grow cactuses. Then he'd rushed off before I could ask him anything. Peter was envious of this weird non-relationship I had with the overseer.

"I have a thousand questions about Nuru history, but he never wants to even look my way," she said. "I'm a married woman *and* I'm here more often than you! What's not to respect? The man is so tall; no one can keep up with his walk, if you see him at all."

Obi and I had grown closer, but further apart. Meaning, we would go out into the desert often with a blanket at sunset and have wonderful passionate sex, but our friendship stagnated. We didn't talk, we didn't give each other gifts, we knew we had no future together. His parents had already betrothed him to a girl from another village who was said to cook the most delicious mushroom soup anyone had ever tasted. It was so tasty that her family sold it and made a decent amount of money on it. The wedding was in a year, which meant Obi and I continued to make the most of his freedom.

He could have contested the engagement and his parents would have listened to him. Obi was close with his parents and he was a level-headed boy. And they knew he loved me. But he didn't contest it and I didn't argue with him. We both knew why it would never work between us. I didn't think anything would ever work between me and *anyone*.

The reason was because of what happened when Obi and I had sex. The first time it happened was not long after I'd returned from the second salt roads journey, when I was fourteen. I'd spent a lot of time on the road flying. My walks were frequent and I took hours to myself, and my brothers and father didn't ask me why I went off alone so often.

Obi and I were so happy to see each other when I came back after that second journey. I don't know what it was, but it was intense and beautiful. We'd met as the sun was going down. It was easy for me to get away, because my brothers were unpacking everything and my father was in the bedroom with my mother telling her some version of how things went that did not include the full truth. I was so glad to get away. Obi was soon to go on the salt roads with his father and five older brothers and everyone was busy, so it was easy for him to get away, too.

We met on the road near the edge of our village. There was no one there but us. When we saw each other, we were both so happy. Everything was changing so quickly. We were growing up, physically, emotionally, in my case spiritually. Our agemates were starting to marry off, many of us were leaving the village, school was starting to not mean as much, yet we were learning so much in our own individual ways. Obi and I hugged for such a long time.

"Najeeeeba!" he said.

"Obi-ooooooo!" I shouted. He smelled like the incense his father was always burning in their home to ward off evil spirits. Whatever had been between us since we were twelve had grown electric. We ran into the desert and, once far enough from our village, the sun down, the stars coming out, we scaled a sand dune, put a blanket down, and stretched out on top of it. There is a freedom amongst the dunes, especially at that hour. There was no fear of being seen or caught. The sky was completely open out here, nothing blocking its presence. The breeze was warm like our bodies. It was dry season, so no flies or mosquitos. And we were young and happy.

We removed all our clothes that evening. The blanket was wide, soft and thick, so no sand got on it. Ah, we'd missed each other. At some point, I worked my way on top of him and I was looking down as I moved over him. He was pulling my hips to his and there was an exquisite sensation. I gasped at the sweetness of it. I moaned. And he moaned and laughed. And then I was standing beside him! I felt hot and I didn't feel like . . . how can I explain it? I had just been as deep in my body as I could be and now I was suddenly outside my body and in another body . . . another sense of being. I was me, but this was a different me.

As I stood there, I realized I was not standing upright but forward. Hot. Glowing, orange-red, yellow. Not small.

"Najeeba?" Obi said, looking up at me.

I made myself smile at him, but I couldn't make my hips move and I couldn't speak. However, my body must have *done* something, because, as I stood there looking at us, Obi's eyes grew wide and his mouth opened. His body tensed and then he breathed, "Oooh . . . Najeeba." I wasn't in my own body when Obi climaxed inside me. For a moment, I stood there in the form I was in. Then I went back into myself. I don't know what Obi must have seen in my eyes as it happened, but he twitched, afraid.

I climbed off and lay beside him as he removed the barrier. He sat up and threw it as far as he could, where it would biodegrade into the sand in minutes. Then we were quiet as we looked at the stars. He suddenly sat up and started putting his clothes back on. "I have to go," he said. I got dressed, too. We didn't speak of it the entire walk back to town. We didn't say a word as we separated and went to our respective homes. I turned for a moment to watch him go. He didn't turn back, walking quickly down the road in the other direction.

And that's how it continued from that point on. Sometimes we spent time with Peter or groups of our classmates. We all laughed and joked, but Obi and I never really laughed and joked with each other anymore. I'd catch Obi looking hard at me, every so often, but that was it. And then at sunsets, every few days, we'd go out in the desert and have sex. And always, when things got intense, I'd leave my body and become the warm glowy thing and Obi would experience some sort of weird power pleasure from me despite the fact that I didn't seem fully present. We both liked it and we both knew something was very wrong with it.

So by the time we were sixteen, Obi and I barely spoke. We were both obsessed with each other for two different reasons. Where I'd always been very lean and flat-chested, that was no longer so much the case. I wasn't what you'd call voluptuous, but I had developed curves. And Obi grew a few more inches and was starting to develop the muscles he'd later become so proud of. He'd begun on the salt roads, lifting salt, walking and sometimes running beside his camel, enjoying the physicality of it all. He kept up with it when he got home.

We had a time, a meeting spot. He brought the blanket, and he always made sure it was sand free. He knew I liked when he smelled of incense and I knew that he liked when I rubbed palm oil on my body. He couldn't get enough of whatever it was that I did to him when I left my body. And I couldn't get enough of what the heat from his body made me become . . . and eventually what I could do. I started to fly as what I was, and time was strange when I was this thing. Between when I left my body and when Obi climaxed, time and space stretched and I could fly far, to other places, where I saw Okeke towns and even Nuru ones.

When I woke up and knew it was time to leave for the salt roads, the knowledge did not surprise or excite me. I chuckled in my bed with my eyes closed, letting myself feel the surety of it. I could see the path in my mind, glowing in the sands like a snake. I was like my father now, not needing to look at my portable to know the way. I paused, opening my eyes. The glowing path in the sands in my mind's eye was the same type of glow as when I changed with Obi into the form that allowed me to travel so far. "Interesting," I whispered. I got up and went to go tell Papa.

He was standing in the center of the sun in the sky room, the large room we'd had added to the house. It was his favorite part of the house now because it got the most sunlight yet somehow stayed wonderfully cool. The sky room was the village hall every two weeks, so there were five couches placed in a circle, the skylight in the center. I sat on one of the couches.

"Sometimes I think you should have been a son," he said.

"But then you wouldn't have a daughter," I said.

He nodded, still holding his face to the sun. "True."

A long silence stretched between us. We had not spoken about two years ago when he'd discovered it was me. He'd never yelled at me for what I'd done, even after we'd made it safely home. However, he'd gone a week without speaking to me, which hurt. I loved being around my father whenever I could, and the absence of that left me feeling even more untethered. And when he'd finally begun speaking to me, he remained cold for weeks before returning to his usual self. My brothers didn't speak of it either. Since then, even after the successful journey last year where I'd performed and earned for the family and village again, in my father's presence, none of us spoke of it.

I started to leave the room.

"Jeeb," he said. "Why?"

"It . . . it took you *two years* to ask me that," I snapped.

"You have never lied to me," he said. "You're my daughter. I was never so ashamed."

"But you spend the money." I motioned around me. "You would not be enjoying this place if it weren't for me, your greatest shame."

"Do you even understand what you have done?" he asked, a pained look on his face.

"Papa, I just . . . I just did it. There was no plotting, conniving, scheming, as I know so many men believe women are constantly doing. Do you really think that of me, Papa?"

"You have always been too impulsive," he said. "I don't know where you get it from. Your mother and I are both careful people."

"Ah, the way I feel when I get up there, Papa. In front of all these buyers . . . it's like . . . I *become*. These words spill from my mouth. Sometimes they rhyme, sometimes they paint beautiful images, because salt is beautiful. You have an eye, Papa, and I describe the things you have an eye for. And people *hear* me. I step out of myself and I let this other part of me step forward. You can't tell me it's wrong."

"It's wrong," my father snapped. He kept his voice down. My mother could not hear this. "You are a *girl*. A young woman soon to be married. If anyone finds out, it doesn't matter how much money we have, no one will want you. And you are already Osu-nu."

I wanted to cry. But instead I kept my voice steady and said, "You were there. You saw. It's not wrong." I walked out of the room and went straight to my garden. I would not go this year or ever again, but I could fly. I dug my hands into the soil, tears welling in my eyes. It wasn't enough. I wanted to be with my father, I wanted to see the dead lake, I could feel the call deep in my heart. I had changed Adoro 5. Girls were going. Why couldn't my father change, too?

"Jeeb?"

I stood up and turned to face my father.

"If your brothers agree, then you can go one more time. Then next year you will marry, and I doubt your husband will want you traveling the salt roads with your father and brothers."

"And will you allow me to speak at the salt market?"

My father refused to make any promises to me. It

was up to my brothers. All of it. My brothers liked money and were both in quiet awe of what I could do. They felt it was a true talent from Ani. What else could a gift so bizarre and profitable be? My mother, not knowing of my market activities, was happy to see me go again. She was proud of me, and she loved the idea of my father, brothers, and me being all together. "It's right," she said. Mama's words and the look on Papa's face when she spoke them made me chuckle to myself.

We left a week later. As usual, it felt wonderful to be on the road. I wasn't sure if Obi would be married by the time I came back. I hadn't wanted to ask. Peter was so happily married that all she wanted to do was talk about her husband and how sweet he was. And this was on the rare occasions she came back to Adoro 5 and I got to spend time with her. I was glad to get away.

The week's journey to the salt mines was peaceful. I went off on my walks, but there was something between my father, brothers, and me that had bloomed. A closeness. It was surprising, and a great relief. Even Ger didn't call his wife much during this time. We laughed and joked, talked about everything. It was quality family time. Once in a while, we even included Mama on Papa's portable . . . though most of the time, she was busy writing or holding community meetings.

During one of the nights we sat around the fire talking, Papa told us that he and the overseer had once gotten very drunk together when they'd shared a table at a friend's wedding.

"All the man would do was laugh, at everything, at everyone," Papa said. "He kept announcing, 'It is all written!'" I had never known my father and the overseer were agemates.

Rayan admitted that his wife snored awfully and the best sleep he had was during this journey. Then he apologized to all of us because such things were only to remain between husband and wife and he meant no disrespect to his wife. Then he burst into tears and my father put an arm around his shoulder and they walked off to talk. As soon as they were gone, Ger rushed up to me. "I'm going with you on your next walk."

I blinked, still trying to process my brother Rayan's outburst about his snoring wife.

"What? Why?"

"Because something is going on with you and I want to know what it is," he said.

"Nothing is . . ." I trailed off and laughed to myself.

He nodded. "I'm coming with you."

"Okay. Fine."

The day before we arrived at the dead lake, we camped at sunset. Ger and I went for a walk while my brother Rayan and my father relaxed by the fire. I'd cooked a large meal of roasted desert hare, cactus stew, dates, and mint tea.

"You cooked all that on purpose," Ger said, as we made our way up a sand dune.

"Yeah," I said.

"You've been doing that," he said.

"You finally noticed."

"I swear, I am beginning to wonder why I ever trusted you with anything all these years. You're not innocent."

"I think that is your issue. You have always assumed I am harmless for some reason." I laughed. "Plus, Mama always taught me that there is power in knowing a man's stomach." We walked until we could not see the camp anymore. We scaled one more sand dune.

"Okay, this is a good spot." I threw down the mat I had brought.

"Good spot for what?" he asked.

"Just sit, Ger."

We sat.

"Now what?" he asked.

A soft breeze was blowing, sand peppering us a bit.

"You have to be open to what I'm . . . I'm going to say. You wanted to come out here."

"Yes. I'm listening."

"You sure you want to know this?"

"Jeeba, I was there that first time you spoke at the market. I saw your face, heard your voice. I've been thinking about it ever since. I want to know."

I looked for a long time into my brother's dark eyes. He was one of the kindest people I knew. Ger had always let me be who I was, even when it was so different from what he was used to. He was a gentle soul, but a curious one, too. I trusted him completely.

"I can do this thing," I said. "It's a thing, but it has forms . . . Sometimes I am this glowing beast. Other times I am just the wind. And at the market, I can project a deep part of myself until it is loud, clear, and forceful . . . but it's all part of the same thing, I believe."

"What in the name of Ani's children are you talking about?"

I sighed. The words were hard to find; this was why

I'd kept them to myself all this time. It was mine. Nevertheless, I eventually found some words. I told him everything as best I could. I am not a storyteller. He asked questions and I answered them. I even told him about having sex with Obi and how it would make me change when I left my body. At first he couldn't help but judge me.

"Don't you want to get married?"

"Of course, but what does that have to do with having sex with Obi?"

"What if you get pregnant?" he said.

"He has always taken the herbs, Gei." I laughed. "What boy his age does not? And we use a barrier."

"You trust him?"

"Always. And do you see me with any baby?"

Then he started asking the interesting questions. "Intercourse makes you become the creature?"

"Maybe. At first. I tried it once, tried to become it on my own . . . It was difficult, but I could see myself starting to glow as I hovered above my body. Then I was pulled back."

"So maybe it was a trigger."

I nodded.

Then finally he asked, "Let me see."

For the first time, I left my body while someone watched, knowing what they were seeing. Obi never understood it. Ger not only understood, but he watched for details. As I left my body, he grabbed my shoulders, looked into my face, looked around. I could see him doing all this. I tried to speak to him as I hovered above him but could not. I flew up high. And there, I stopped thinking about what my brother was doing and I focused on myself. I was thinking about the form I often took with Obi. I tried to become it now. I was nothing but what I perceived to be a swirl of air, breeze. I could rush past a tree and rustle its leaves, I could whirl around and gently kick up dust, or I could be so still that I affected nothing.

I tried to be more. On purpose. Heat. The glow of a fire one sees with one's peripheral vision, the sun just after it has set. "Shades of fire," I said aloud in my windy voice. I thought about one of the books the overseer had given me. There was a lizard in the desert that thrived around a certain type of cactus. It would sun itself at that cactus's highest point. This lizard was said to be all the shades of fire. The book said that when this lizard dreamed, it took its truest form at the hottest point in the day. The size of four camels, lean and strong like a snake, coiled horns, magnificent jaw. *"Kponyungo,"* I said, remembering the name. And the moment I spoke the word, I became.

I gasped, my eyes focusing. There was a sand grain in my left eye. I blinked it out. I hadn't been trying to return to myself. I'd been the creature. But only for a moment. Then I was looking into my brother's face. He looked just as surprised as me. "Are you back?" he nearly shouted. "Najeeba?!"

"I am. I am." I leaned back as he sat back, staring at me.

"I don't even know what to call what I just witnessed," he said.

I laughed. "Try."

He shook his head. "You weren't completely gone." He frowned. "Did you truly go?"

"Yes. I flew way up high."

"You just seemed drowsy. And you kept trying to talk, but you couldn't speak words."

"Could you sense when I left? Tell me as much as you can. Obi never says anything."

"I felt you shudder, but only slightly. I . . . did hear . . . there was a sort of whoosh. It went up! Then you just sat there, a smile on your face, eyes open, blinking like normal. But you *felt* cooler. But just before you came back, you felt hot!"

Kponyungo, I thought. What was it to be one of those? And why?

"Ani is great," he whispered.

"She is great," I recited.

After a moment, he asked, "Why? What is this?"

"I don't know."

"It does not seem bad," he said, looking out into the desert.

"No."

"Well, Najeeba, you are my sister and I love you. Anything Ani gifts you with shall prosper. It says so in the Great Book. Rayan and Papa agree, too. That's why you are here. That's why you will sell all our salt at the market." He gave me a tight hug and I felt like crying. Then he held me back and said, "But it is some sort of mystics, juju. The spirits know you." He brought out his portable and looked at the time. "We should get back."

I nodded.

======

CHAPTER 8

In the Pink

We reached the dead lake by midday the next day. We set up where we usually set up, about a half mile from where the ground was flat and saltless. I unfolded the raffia trough and filled it with water for the camels using the capture station. My brothers unloaded the camels, who rushed over to drink from the trough. My father put on his sunglasses and went up a sand dune to scope out the dead lake. Something about the way he stood and looked over the dead lake reminded me of me when I was about to leave my body.

Papa was walking back to us when he stopped and brought his portable from his pocket. I could hear him talking to my mother on it. My portable could not communicate with anyone the way my father's portable could. I was glad Papa's could do this out of all of ours. Mama liked to be alone, but that connection to Papa and therefore the rest of us was so necessary.

Papa's camel Dusty was drinking so loudly that I could not hear what Papa was saying, but he was suddenly pressing his hand to his forehead. My brothers, who were closer to him, had stopped what they were doing to look at him. My father turned his back to us and started walking away.

"Ger, Rayan, what is it?" I asked.

They were already rushing to him. I did, too.

"There is nothing you can do from there, my love," Mama was saying when I got within earshot.

"Should . . . should we . . ."

"No," my mother said sternly.

"What did they take?" my father asked.

My brothers looked stunned.

"What?" I shouted. "What happened?" *And was it my fault?* I wondered.

Papa glanced at me, his eyes wide. He turned, walking steps away. My mother was talking quickly. "It doesn't matter now, just . . ."

"Rayan, what's going on?" I asked. I caught Ger's eye.

"The Paper House was attacked," Rayan said.

"By whom?"

He shrugged. "Okekes who feel 'untouchables' don't have the right to collect knowledge."

In the past, such attacks had happened. Sometimes even Nurus would set upon our communities to take what they felt belonged to them, for everything an Okeke owned belonged to the Nuru. And when Nuru came, they usually left many dead and none free. But not in my lifetime. Other Okekes usually just left us alone as long as the only time they saw us was at the market selling our salt. "Was anyone hurt?" I asked.

"Kelechi Odumi," Ger said.

I looked at him questioningly. I didn't know the name.

"The overseer," he added.

"Oh no!"

"They beat him badly . . . They even broke his arm," Rayan said. He went to my father, who'd walked halfway back up the dune.

Ger and I looked at each other, the question hanging between us: Was the attack over?

We were a week's journey away from home. He stepped over and hugged me close and I wept quietly into his chest. After a few moments he tapped on my shoulder. I could hear my brother, Papa, and Mama all talking quietly from afar. "Jeeba," Ger said. "Can you . . . go and see?" I froze, my cheek still to his chest. I hadn't considered such a thing. Could I *do* such a thing?

"I don't know," I whispered. "It's so far."

"You've gone farther," he said. "Mama won't tell Papa if it's unsafe," he said. "She wouldn't want us to come back right away."

I glanced at Rayan and Papa. They were huddled together as they talked to Mama. "Go to them. Keep them away from me for as long as you can," I said.

"Okay." He rushed to Papa and Rayan.

I went to where the camels were drinking and sat on a bundle of supplies, out of Papa and Rayan's line of sight. I stared toward the dead lake, sparkling in the distance. It was easy to find what I needed to leave my body here. I'd seen plenty of witches whirling about the dead lake since I'd started coming here. I flew up and away, no moment to revel in the joy of what I was doing. I found the kponyungo faster than I'd ever found it. Heat. Glow. I was the serpent-like beast and I flew fast, unbothered by space and unhindered by time. Only a need to see to Mama and my home. I crumpled time like paper. I didn't know how I did it and, at the moment, I didn't care. I had to do it; that was all that mattered. So I did it.

I streaked across the desert. Would I be able to return to my body? I didn't think about that either. And then I was home. High above our house, looking down through the sky-room window. There was Mama. I flew down. There were others. The house was full. Village leaders, men and women, some children. I flew to the huge sky-room window. However, while it had been easy enough to get here, now that I was here, it was suddenly like moving through honey.

My body was trying to pull me back. I resisted and pulled myself closer to the window.

". . . perimeter around Adoro 5," our village chief Unoma was saying. She stood in the middle of the room, turning as she spoke so that she could make eye contact with everyone. "We will be ready for anyone who tries to come here again. Spread the word that we are secure. And so far, there is no sign of further attack."

"Why would they come back? They made off with almost everything in the Paper House," schoolteacher Teodros said.

"We *will* replenish the Paper House again," Chief Unoma swore.

I retreated. The pull was unbearable and I'd heard what I needed. But there was one more thing. The pull lessened for a moment, as if it were giving me a little more time. I walked down the road, feeling like a great beast. No one was outside, so I could not tell if anyone saw or sensed me. I hoped I'd see the village cat, but it was nowhere in sight, either. I arrived at the Paper House and got barely a glimpse of it before whatever was pulling me yanked me so hard that home retreated from me in a wink.

I grunted as I found myself staring into Abdul's nostrils as he sniffed at my face. I fell backward off the bundle off supplies I'd been sitting on. "Oof!" Then a great headache slammed into my head. "Ah!" I clapped my hands to my temples. I slowly stood up and stumbled toward Abdul. He didn't move, allowing me to lean on his water-filled belly. I rested my head there, as the pain grew and then began to retreat. When I opened my eyes, I saw black spots and I had to blink away tears. "Ger!" I called. I slurred his name and it sounded more like "Grrrrr." I rubbed my eyes. The spots had faded but weren't completely gone. Papa, Rayan, and now Ger were all still huddled together.

Ger saw me and came running over. "You all right?" He grabbed my shoulder to hold me up.

"Will be," I said. The spots were almost gone. "I did it."

"You went?"

I nodded. "It's over for now."

"So we should stay?"

I nodded.

"Mama?"

"She's telling the truth. She was in the sky room with what looked like half of Adoro 5."

Ger looked hard at me. "You were really *there*?"

"I don't think I should do anything like that again anytime soon."

"No," he said, looking me over.

"They set the inside on fire," I blurted. "What they didn't take, they tried to burn."

He stared at me. Clearly Mama had not said anything about that. The pride of Adoro 5 had been mostly destroyed.

"We can't leave," I said. "Not without bringing back money to help rebuild and restock."

"Oh," Ger said, understanding. "You are right."

The next day, before any of us got up, Papa took a water carrier and went off alone into the dead lake. He said nothing to any of us, but we knew what he was doing and we knew why. Papa was the one who had the eye for special salt cubes, but most of the time we went on the search together. However, the stakes were higher now. He *needed* to find something unique that I could sell for a high cost and he didn't have the luxury of taking his time doing it. He searched best while alone. He may have also needed time alone. He was fond of the overseer and maybe the entire incident had made old wounds ache. Papa didn't take well to threats to his family. Being so far away from Mama had shaken him.

An hour later, I went with my brothers to gather salt cubes. We didn't talk much, and I took the time to think about how I'd flown home, so far and so specific. I wasn't just exploring, I'd imagined the place and gone straight there. This was different than just flying over the dead lake and seeing what was out there on a fun whim. I'd seen home. Mama. I had known what I was doing was real, but this made it even more so. And when I'd returned, my brain and mind had been more addled than when I drank too much palm wine at Water Fest.

By sundown, we'd collected as much salt as the camels could carry. We'd load the camels in the morning and head out early. What we'd found wasn't the most quality salt; there was no time for that. It was all up to Papa and we knew it. None of us could do what he could do. However, Papa still wasn't back yet.

"Should we go out and look for him?" I asked.

"No," Rayan snapped. "Where would we start? At this hour? His portable cannot be tracked here. We'll all just get lost and waste more time."

"So we just stay here?" I asked. "What if he's—"

Ger pointed at me. "Don't speak those words."

"But—"

"We stay *here*," Rayan said. "Papa knows this place better than we do."

We built a fire and soon it was dark. None of us could eat. I considered flying out to look for him. In the dark, I would just look asleep. And though Rayan wouldn't know, Ger would, and would maybe even make excuses for me. But then Dusty, my father's camel, stood up and turned toward the dead lake. We all scrambled to our feet, looking into the darkness. There was a light from far away. It was pink.

"Papa?" I shouted.

For a moment, there was no answer. Then, faintly, I heard, "Come and see!" Papa was much farther than we thought. We used our portables to light our way as we rushed to him, stepping over old roots and around stunted shrubs. As my brothers and I got closer, whatever he was using for light grew stronger.

"What is that?" Rayan called.

"It's not his portable," I said, out of breath.

My father was laughing when we reached him. He was blackened by the sun and dirty with dust. But he was laughing. He carried his empty water carrier over his shoulder and only one other item: a glowing, perfectly shaped cube of salt in his arms, the size of a large monkey breadfruit. "I have found it," my father said.

"What is it?" Rayan asked, taking it from him.

Our father tiredly bent forward and stretched his back as he loudly grunted with relief. "Thank you, my son!" Then he sat down right there on the dirt, exhausted. "It is what will save Adoro 5, our great village."

Rayan put it on the ground in front of Papa and the three of us crowded around it. It looked like the most transparent cube of salt I'd ever seen. Utterly pure. Except . . . it glowed pink. Something was in its center. Round like a tiny planet. I could see the thing slowly rotating and flickering into a slightly different shade of pink. I tapped on the cube. It was solid and cool.

The light it gave off wasn't warm, despite being powerful. It lit the entire area. Even from where we were, I could see our camp and, in the other direction, the shine of salt crystals from the beginnings of the dead lake.

Ger pressed the side of his head to it, listening. "It hums," he said.

"How did you find it?" Rayan asked. "And let's get you back to camp."

"In a moment," Papa said, dismissively waving a hand. "I am fine. Just tired. I hiked farther than I have ever gone. There was a very big crater, like something had smashed the land. The ground there was thick with dust—not dirt, but pulverized salt, I think. It was white and very very fine. My feet left prints. I saw a few footprints from birds, as well. Large ones, maybe a vulture or hawk. I covered my mouth with my veil. I did not want to breathe what my feet sent into the air. There were several cubes near the bottom of the crater that glowed like this. I only took one."

"Take only what you need," Rayan recited.

Papa nodded. "Take only what you need." He touched the cube. "Plus, there was this feeling there. No . . . not a feeling, a memory. The place made me remember." He shook his head. "I don't know. You all know the story in the Great Book, how Ani brought the Nuru from the stars, that when she did, first she brought the cleansing starlight. I was seeing the starlight in this place. How the lake died and the salt we live on came to be. That place held the memory of it all. So much memory . . ." He tapered off and rubbed his dirty face.

"Papa," Rayan said. "We have a long day tomorrow. Let's get you back."

He nodded and allowed Ger and me to help him up. He leaned on us the entire way, Rayan walking ahead of us, carrying the cube. As we walked, I wondered if I heard the hum of the cube, too. Except what I was hearing sounded more like whispers. I shivered, despite the warmth of Papa's body.

CHAPTER 9

On the Road

The cube glowed even in the sunshine. I don't know why this was a surprise to me, but it was.

"Do you have any idea what it is?" I asked as my father affixed the leather strap he was using to carry the cube to the knob at the front of Dusty's saddlebag.

"Who can know the dead lake and what it produces?" he said. "But the Great Book mentions the releasing of 'mysterious mysticisms' upon Ani's awakening. 'The end of Okeke technology ushered in other technologies.'"

Then maybe we should leave it here, I thought, only fleetingly. Papa was right, the pink cube would fetch a price so high that we'd be able to use the money to restock the Paper House.

"I wonder what the salt will taste like when it's ground up," Rayan said.

"Anyone brave enough to put a grate to that thing, let alone *taste* the grated salt, is also a fool," Ger said.

Papa looked stern as he said, "That will be up to the buyer."

"It will either cure or kill," Ger muttered, climbing onto his reluctantly sitting camel Suad.

"Not our concern," Papa said.

Ger's camel groaned loudly as she stood up. He rubbed her long neck. "Until they come to Adoro 5 for revenge."

"Then it will be war," Papa said. "No one is responsible for what the salt does except the buyer."

"But in this case—"

"Enough," Papa snapped, urging Dusty to start walking.

It would take us days to reach the market. The going was through dry hills, and between those hills lurked powerful witches. They'd whip up suddenly, but never directly on us. To me this was more testament that witches were sentient. Inside some of the hills were caves. These caves could be surprisingly cool inside, even at the height of the day. If the heat grew too intense, we rested inside them for the day and set out at night. Night travel was best for the camels, but things lurked in the night that made day travel a better choice. That was just fact.

Still, this fateful day, a little less than two days away from the market, just before we began to see other caravans heading in the same direction, was an exceptionally hot day. I cannot tell you how hot it was because our portables all shut themselves off. Even in my weather-treated clothes, I was beginning to feel uncomfortable.

"Kai!" Rayan exclaimed. "Ani is trying to turn us all into ash today!"

Papa was looking behind him, and I looked, too. He'd been doing that for the last hour.

"Do you see someone, Papa?" I asked.

"No . . . just . . ." He looked at me and I couldn't read his face because he was all veiled up.

"It's probably nothing. Let's stop for the day. Night will have to do."

"That cave looks perfect," Ger said, pointing, as if he'd been waiting for Papa to give in.

The cave was sizable, big enough to fit all of us, including the camels. And it was clean. No other animals had made this place their home in some time. While everyone settled on their mats, I did a once-over for spiders, lizards, and anything else that may have been lurking in this place. I didn't mind spiders, but lizards bothered me. All I found was one large spider, and it was set up near the top of the cave, not disturbing anyone. I unrolled my mat at the back of the cave and there I played my Dark Shadows game for a while.

A breeze picked up. Ger started a cooking fire in a large circle of rocks in the shade, on which he placed a pot of rice to cook. Having had enough of my Dark Shadows game, I leaned back on my elbows, gazing at the craggy cave ceiling. At some point, my brothers and Papa gathered around the fire and began to sing old songs. I couldn't see from where I was, but I suspect they were smoking, because their singing grew wilder and wilder, plus I could smell the sweet floral fragrance of the smoke. I heard stamping feet. I think my brother Rayan was dancing.

He always danced when he smoked.

I let my eyes unfocus, listening to their joy and feeling the warm breeze on my skin. Mama was all right at home. We had the pink cube and it was going to save Adoro 5 and what it earned would make the Paper House into more than it had ever been. My belly was full of dates, spiced rice, and what remained of the roasted meat. For the moment, I was content.

I began to rise from my body. It was a good time to do it. I would travel ahead and see what was going on at the market. It was past midnight, and the night market would be in full swing. Merchants would be selling mysterious old tech pulled from caves and the type of weed that when eaten right after sex made a woman conceive, Ewu women would be coaxing adventurous men into the shadows, and storytellers would tell news only the brave could bear to hear.

And this was how I saw it begin from far above the cave. And I heard it as if it were right beside me. A deep intake of breath. My father was dancing. My brothers were standing there, arms over each other's shoulders, watching my father, laughing. As my father danced, he stamped up dust. But the dust wasn't settling. I remember this specifically because I'd stopped flying away, turned back and watched. The dust was not settling. I saw all this in what felt like minutes, but time is different when I travel. It may have been seconds. Dusty was sitting in the shade, just at the lip of the cave. The cube was in its leather strap beside him. It was broad daylight, yet I could see the cube glowing. Like a lesser sun.

There was someone standing in the entrance of the cave. Between me and my family. A man? He was facing them. I could not see from so high up. But a ripple of terror flew through me despite the fact that my body was below.

I flew back. I opened my eyes. For a moment, they would not focus.

Immediately, I was breathing heavily, my body full of adrenaline. I was in the shade of the cave. I scrambled shakily to my feet, glad that I was already wearing my sandals. I stepped around the corner.

Who was that in the cave entrance? A man. Tall. He wore tattered robes that could have been yellow or had been white once. The dusty wind blew around him as he watched my brothers and father. Papa was still dancing wildly, flinging his arms this way and that. My brothers were clapping and urging him on. They did not notice the man standing there. I grasped the cave's wall as the man suddenly began to ululate.

Was he actually there? I realized there was *another* man standing outside the cave, in the dust, yards away from Papa and my brothers! There was another! Some old, some younger, Nuru, Okeke, other, I could not tell. Maybe I was too afraid to look at their faces too closely. I didn't want to see their eyes. They sparkled in their dirty robes. They wore sandals and dirty pants like the first man I'd seen. Their wooly hair was caked with dust as it blew in what was now a dusty wind. How did Papa and my brothers not see them all?

A hum. The camels grew restless, moving farther back into the cave, toward me. I crept beside Abdul. My brothers and Papa finally noticed them.

"Who are you!?" Ger shouted.

"Ah! Get back!" Papa said, pushing my brothers behind him, toward the fire. He reached into his pocket, pulled out a pouch of salt, poured some into his hand, and threw it at the one closest to him. The grains bounced off the man's garments.

"Haaaaaah," the man breathed at Papa. It sounded like pleasure.

Rayan tried to move around our father. "No, Rayan!" Papa snapped. He glanced at the cube near Abdul. "They're not people!" His eyes found me. He quickly looked away, addressing one of the men. "Leave us be!"

No . . . not men. As I crept closer, I saw that they may have been shaped like adult male human beings, but they were not. Their flesh was not well, their legs and arms were mismatched, their expressionless faces twitched with unnatural animation. They did not walk; they shuffled toward him, as if they would fall apart if they tried to move any faster.

Yet the wind did not affect them at all. Their garments did not blow. The gusts of wind only made them insubstantial, only for them to become whole moments later. The humming grew louder as they moved closer. Now there were at least twenty of them. All in front of the cave. My brothers and Papa pressed closer together.

Was I supposed to sit and watch these creatures tear apart my family? But who was I? I had no weapons, and there were too many of them. I was just a girl. They were terrifying. What even *were* they? Rayan was the first to attack. He moved around my father and threw a punch at the one closest to him. There was a burst of dust from within its garments as my brother's punch went into its face. Then one of its arms thrust out and whacked my brother aside. He fell a foot from the cooking fire, holding his shoulder as blood ran from his nose.

"Get back!" Papa screamed at them as he rushed to Rayan. "In the name of Ani."

Ger stood there unprotected by Papa, shaking. Another grabbed and pulled at him. He hollered in pain as he was yanked away. He couldn't fight them at all; they were that powerful. Another grabbed Rayan and dragged him away, leaving our father with the rest of them closing in on him. Clearly, Papa was who they wanted. But what for?

I stepped out of the cave. Not one turned my way. Then I did all I knew how to do. I'd never considered it before, but when your father is about to be pulled apart by what looks like desert spirits, a lot of new things go through your mind. One of them grabbed him by the throat and began pulling his face to its filthy garments. I heard Papa's muffled cries. I dropped to Abdul's legs. I looked at him and said, "Protect me." He was still staring at me as I left.

I flew upward and, as I did, I became the kponyungo. But not to travel. And I could see and feel myself more strongly than ever. My hefty reptilian body was long and coily. My head was rectangular with thick arching horns that ran its length. My mouth was full of sharp teeth. Thin smoke tumbled from my red-orange, smoky, ethereal flesh, trailing behind me.

I flew at them. In this form, I could smell them.
They smelled chemical. Like the acrid smoke of a broken capture station that has not been turned off. The
whole place stank of them. The whispery hum I'd been
hearing since Papa brought the pink cube was louder.
I imagined this sound in my throat and then I blew it
at them. Hot flames. They burst apart as if they were
made of explosives. Maybe it was the intense heat, the
wind, the dryness of their garments, whatever mys-
teries they were made of, that I was made of, their an-
imated death, the desert. Maybe it was all those things.
They became fire, then collapsed into ash and smoke.
I could see right through the dust. There were more
creatures on the other side of the cave. All around it.
I blew fire on all of them as I flew. I blew until they
were gone. I could not see my brothers or Papa in the
dust, ash, and smoke, but I could see the cube glowing its relentless pink. Its intensity decreased as I blew
away the spirit creatures.

When they were gone, I flew all around for a while
longer. Making sure, yet still unsure. Gradually, I came
back to myself. *What did I just do?* My throat ached
and I was glowing. I could see myself, lizard-like,
snake-like, scaled, the color of flames. Kponyungo.

My brothers were holding my father up. But not like yesterday. He was not laughing with the sweet exhaustion of success. His mouth hung open, dribbling saliva. I returned to my body, coughing. Abdul had sat down beside me and I leaned on his body. He *had* protected me. I shuddered, trying to quickly adjust. No time to adjust. I tried to get up and fell to the side, wracked with coughs from all the dust and ash and smoke. My eyes watered and my nose ran. "Papa!" I screamed, stumbling to the front of the cave. I fell to my knees, coughing. I dragged myself up, using the side of the cave. "Papa! Rayan! Ger!"

"Over here!" Ger shouted. "Come on!"

The wind was beginning to blow the dust away, and I could see my brothers. Moving from the cave, carrying Papa, who barely seemed conscious. We all collapsed some yards outside the cave.

"Is he all right?" I asked, crawling over to them.

The wind blew away the last of the strange dust, and now it was dying down. The sun was beginning to set, its intensity finally subsiding.

"Don't know," Rayan said, laying our father out. He knelt over him and patted his cheek.

"Papa?"

Papa coughed and blinked tears. "Dust in my eyes."

"Want to sit up?" Rayan asked. Papa nodded. We all helped him to sit up. He coughed some more and leaned against Ger. We stayed like this for a long time. Leaning on each other, afraid to move.

The spirit creatures did not return. But the cube continued to glow. By night, it was lighting the camp as we packed up. Papa was still weak, so he sat on his camel as we strapped everything back onto the other camels. The last item was the pink cube.

"I'm not touching that thing," Papa muttered. He hadn't said anything in two hours.

"I'll carry it on Abdul," I said.

"Let's leave it here," Papa said, his voice cracking. "Kelechi forgive me, ooo!" He sadly shook his head. Even now he thought of the overseer and the Paper House's well-being.

My siblings and I looked at each other, unsure. It was night, and if these things had come because of the pink cube and they came back in the night, we'd never survive. Unless I blew them all away again. "Papa," I said. "Let's finish what we started. We are not far and soon there will be other caravans."

"It was that cube that brought them," he said. "I shouldn't have captured it." He rubbed his face, his eyes still watering. I didn't know if it was dust still in his eyes or tears.

"Captured," Papa had said. As if it were a living thing. We were all quiet again as we thought about it. What if the spirit creatures simply killed us and all the caravans? Who would really know? Or care? Stranger things have happened in the desert, especially on the salt roads."

"I think Najeeba is right," Ger said. "I think it may be because we stopped, too. Let us keep moving. We won't stop until we get there."

"We have to try," I added.

"Papa?" Rayan asked.

"Fine," Papa said, sounding defeated.

We traveled through the night. Even with my skill of sleeping on camels, I did not sleep. We didn't talk about what had happened. I don't know about Papa and my brothers, but to me, talking about it felt like a sure way of calling the spirits back. The cube lit the night world all around us. So if the creatures returned, we would, at least, see them coming. When we took some time to rest, I stayed close and even slept right beside Papa, my brothers on the other side. We didn't talk much, and when we did, we only used low voices. We didn't want them to hear us, either. Thankfully, they did not come back, and soon we were traveling with hundreds of other caravans on their way to the market. We'd wrapped the pink cube in more leather so we wouldn't attract attention.

The next day was not nearly as hot, and I was beginning to wonder if the heat had had something to do with what had happened, even if that didn't make any sense. The sun was preparing to set when we finally approached the lights and noise of the market. We found a nice open area to camp on, and it was when Papa climbed down that I noticed he was still not recovered from whatever the creature had done to him.

He looked tired and his brown skin had a gray undertone and his eyes were bloodshot.

He got off his camel slowly and stretched his back. He was out of breath. "We are here," he said.

"We are here," the three of us repeated.

"Papa," Rayan said. "How do you feel?"

Papa looked about to say he felt fine, but then he sighed. "I feel bad."

We all laughed at his truthfulness. It was not like Papa to lie. So at least he was still *acting* like himself.

Rayan nodded. "You *look* bad. Let us handle everything. We'll set up our tent and you can wash and then rest."

The next day, I wrapped myself in my garments and put on my face veil. Papa stayed in our tent and the three of us used Dusty and Abdul to carry our salt. Then we went to the salt market.

CHAPTER 10

Passing

"Are you ready?" Rayan asked, once we were set up. We kept the pink cube in the leather.

I nodded. I was more than ready. I was excited. Plus, I had a solid reason to take this risk. The image of my tired father bubbled up in my head and I caught my breath. Then those spirit creatures. What had they done to him? And would it pass? It *had* to pass. I looked over the salt market. People were already gathering. Many had been waiting for us to set up for the past half hour. I placed a hand on the wrapped-up pink cube. I could smell the leather. My father had had these pieces for many years, using them for miscellaneous reasons. Never would I have thought they'd be used to cover a piece of mystical salt from the dead lake.

I was sixteen years old now. Taller. More confident. I'd done this several times already and each time I'd made a fortune. These people knew me now, even if they didn't know me. I was a girl. They thought I was a boy. It didn't matter. I could become something that charmed them into spending all their money. And they never left disappointed. They gained from buying from me. I unwrapped the pink cube.

There was a gasp from people around us. I waited. More people gathered. Rayan pushed a stool beside me. I looked at him and he smiled. "Use what Ani gave you," he whispered. I stepped onto the stool. I took a deep breath, and when I looked up, I felt myself split into two. I lifted above myself and I faced the crowd. "This is the most valuable item you will ever see," I said. "And it is for sale."

I sold every cube we had, first. Most could not afford the pink cube, but they wanted to have salt that was etched with "Xabief Enterprises." When I got to the pink cube, the entire salt market was at our space, pressing in. Rayan and Ger stood on each side of the cube, but there was really nothing to worry about. There was a code of trust in the salt market that was a century old. To steal salt was to curse one's bloodline forever.

I don't remember the exchange at all. It was at this moment that I was flying high above the market. I flew over our camp. Father was in the tent, most likely asleep. I flew beside a vulture riding the thermals. It seemed to know I was there, and we danced around and around each other for what felt like hours. I was the kponyungo and I was glowing brilliantly. Then I was called and I came back to myself. The woman was walking away. A woman in the salt market. A richly dressed Okeke woman who smelled of perfumed oils. She was carrying the pink cube and she was followed by a procession of Okeke women, also richly dressed. The entire market had stopped everything and was staring at them, and no one said a word or got in their way. There were three men standing in front of me. Rayan and Ger were on both sides of me.

Ger was loading sacks and sacks onto Abdul.

"I don't know what you're talking about," Rayan was hissing at one of the men.

"I can see it with my own eyes," the man said. He wore no face veil, but his garments were all a rich blue, which went well with his blue-black skin. "You have what you came here for. Now leave before there is trouble."

The man standing beside him stepped up close to me and looked me in the face. "And never bring *her* back."

My eyes widened. They knew. I frowned and looked at my feet, ashamed. It had crossed my mind earlier this year. I was still lean, but I had developed over the last year. I now had breasts and a proper backside. Even my facial structure had shifted. Then I'd pushed the thought away, not feeling like dealing with it. I still wore my blue face veil.

"I resent what you are implying," Rayan sneered, pushing me behind him.

"I resent *you* scamming us all these years," the man said.

The man beside him pulled him back. "Leave these people. At least that evil thing was sold from one witch to another. Let them deal with it."

"Yes, because they outbid *you*," Ger shot back.

The men turned to him. Then they turned to me. The taller one smirked. He pointed me out and turned to the salt market. Most had left, but plenty of people were selling salt and thus easily within earshot.

"Get moving," Rayan shouted at Ger. Ger started leading Abdul and Dusty away.

"Salt sellers and buyers! Do you know who this one who has been selling to you all these years for the highest price is? This one we all know from Xabief Enterprises? Do you wonder why Xabief himself is never here to do the sales? Why he lets this sweet-tongued boy trick us into emptying our pockets?! We trust these Osu-nu people far too much."

Rayan stayed, but I was scrambling away just behind Ger. I didn't get far. The shorter man ran and grabbed me and pulled me right back to where I'd been standing. He yanked off my face veil. "This is not a boy, this is a *woman*!"

Once the spell of assumption is broken, it cannot be recast. For the second time, I heard a gasp ripple through the market. Followed by shouts of outrage.

"Abomination!" someone said.

I heard Rayan shout to Ger to keep going. Then there was chaos. A press of bodies.

People grabbing at me. Men.

"A female selling in the market!"

"Liar!"

"Osu-nu witch!"

"Rayan," I shouted.

"Najeeba!" But his voice was too far from me.

Someone grabbed at my breast. I shoved him away, putting my hand to his face. I could feel the roughness of his beard and mustache and his nose mashing beneath my fingers. Someone punched me and I stumbled to the side. Everything went strange for a moment. Then Rayan was trying to drag me along. Then he wasn't there and I felt hands grab my shoulders, my waist. I screamed. These were the people who had a century-old "code" that prevented stealing. I fell. I heard laughter as I was shoved this way and that. I fell to my knees in the dirt and tasted blood in my mouth.

Someone hit me in the head.

Stomped on my leg.

Blackness. Just for a moment.

I was flying from my body. Was it as a kponyungo or something more primal? I will never know. I was not in my right mind. And I was so angry. I hurt so badly. I burst forth. I was not flying; this was a violence, a rage, a fury. All around. I saw and felt flames. I heard myself roaring, though it did not feel like it came from my mouth, my thought. It came from my pained body.

When I returned to myself, people were fleeing.

Leaving their wares. Falling over each other. To get away from me. Even Rayan. I stood there, watching it all. I coughed, sitting on the ground. My nose was bleeding, my chest and the side of my head ached, my calf was starting to swell up. There is no feeling like sitting in the dirt watching an entire market of men, fleeing from you. I felt like an abomination. I was an abomination.

But, oh Ani, I was so powerful.

They would talk about it for many years. I suspect it is still legend to this day. No one was hurt, but everyone who was there, including my brothers, was plagued with nightmares of flames and heat. The sweet-tongued boy-who-was-actually-a-woman of Xabief Enterprises was possessed by evil spirits.

We fled, Ger pushing Abdul and Dusty into a trot, despite the crowds. He looked at me as Rayan and I caught up with him. All around us, people were running. Few were paying attention to us as news of what happened back in the salt market spread. People assumed we were still back there. "What did you . . ."

"I don't know!" I said.

"Shut up and keep going!" Rayan said.

When we reached our father, he was still sleeping,

more lethargic than ever. "Papa," I asked, turning my face away so he would not see that it was swollen and bloody. "Are you all right?"

"Did you do it?" he whispered.

"Yes, Papa." I wiped my face with a piece of cloth.

"How much?"

"We have to *go!*"

He laughed tiredly. "That much, huh?"

We managed to get him on his camel, though Rayan had to strap him on with the leather from the pink cube. We were on our way in minutes. I winced with every step my camel Abdul took, but I kept up, trying not to look around too much. People were still going to the salt market to see what had happened. A few people looked hard at us, and I knew they recognized us, but they kept going.

"Thank goodness it'll be a year before we go back again," Ger said an hour later, the market in the distance.

"If we ever go again," Rayan said.

They both looked at me. Then we looked at Papa.

By the end of the day, it was clear that we were being followed. They stayed about a mile away, but they had been behind us for quite some time. Papa was still out of it and this scared me. If we had to flee, how was he going to keep up? Even the leather straps wouldn't hold him on a running camel.

"What do you have?" Rayan asked. He'd brought out his machete. Ger held up a dagger and brass knuckles. I didn't have anything. No, that was not true. I had my kponyungo and whatever I'd done back at the market. I had plenty. There'd been no time to tell my brothers what I'd done, so I'd have to play damsel in distress while I caused chaos.

"Abdul," I said, patting him on the neck. "Protect me again?"

When the sun was nearly set, we stopped and camped near a large stone jutting from the ground. The people following us camped nearby, building a large fire. They weren't trying to hide their presence at all. Abdul rested, but we kept the bags of money near enough to his back to quickly load. Our other supplies we unpacked. Except the capture stations. One could find food in the desert, even in the harshest part, but water was life. We were ready if we had to flee quickly. Sort of. Papa, who was still weak, though he was growing stronger and more aware, lay on his mat, propped up by one of our supply sacks.

"Who did you sell the pink cube to?" he asked me as I handed him a plate of dates and roasted meat.

I sprinkled some salt on the meat and we both whispered, "Salt is life." Then I said, "An Osu-nu elite from somewhere I'd never heard of."

My father's eyebrows went up. He took a pinch of the salt on his plate and rubbed it between his fingers, holding his plate with his other hand. "I have never met one anywhere. But an elite at the salt market? That's even more unexpected. Are you sure she was?"

"Yes," Ger said. "She was a woman who had no fear of being there. And no other Okeke could have the amount of money she paid. And she had the tribal markings. All the way up each arm. I looked at them closely."

We were all about to go to sleep when we saw the light coming toward us. Not the powerful light of the pink cube, but the weak light of a portable. I moved behind my brothers, away from our fire, into the shadows. I touched the bruise on the side of my head; I couldn't take another beating. Papa slowly got to his feet. Where my brothers each grabbed their weapons, he did not bother.

There were three of them. All Nuru, wearing the rough clothes of those who traveled most of the time. "Nuru nomads," I muttered to myself.

The one who led the way looked like he only ate when he was nearly dead. In the firelight, his face still pale even after so much desert sunlight scared me. Gaunt, his cheekbones reminded me of a skeleton, and he was smiling. "Xabief of Xabief Enterprises," he said, spreading his arms.

"That is me," Papa said, walking to them. My brothers moved close to him.

"Congratulations on your salt sales," the man said.

"Who are you, and why are you coming to my camp speaking of my business at night, unannounced?" Papa asked.

"Apologies," he said. "I am Cat, and I am not here to see you."

"Then leave."

"A sorcerer goes where he pleases."

I heard Ger gasp. Rayan elbowed him. My father said nothing.

"What do you want?"

But the man who called himself Cat stepped around Papa. He pointed right at me in the dark. The gesture scared me so deeply that I twitched backward, my back pressing against Abdul.

"You, girl, woman," he said striding toward me. I nearly ran away. My father and brothers came after him. He brought up a hand and immediately they stopped—quiet, frozen.

I turned and faced him.

"Leave us alone," I said.

"Or you'll what?" he asked. "Try it again."

I knew better. Plus, I could not even if I wanted to. I was not angry, I was terrified. My father and brothers were just standing there because he'd *done* something to them. Oh, I just wanted to go *home*. I wanted my mother.

He stood looking at me and me looking at him. His eyes were wild but calculating. He was wholly silent. The two men who'd come with him stood where they'd stopped, just outside our camp. "Looks like they taught you a lesson," Cat said. "But will you learn?" Then he raised a hand and stretched all his fingers wide. Something flew from it to me. I felt it hit me in the forehead. It felt wet and itchy. I resisted the urge to rub at the spot. He turned and walked off, the two other men he'd come with following him. When they were nearly halfway to their camp, my father and brothers were able to move. Rayan shouted curses at him,

Ger sunk to the ground relieved, and my father just watched them go. Then he turned to me.

"Are you all right?"

"Yes," I said. "Are you?"

"I'm feeling better," he said.

CHAPTER 11

She Who Knows

They did not come back. I used the capture station to gather a whole sack of water so I could bathe more thoroughly than I had since we'd left home. I scrubbed and scrubbed my forehead. The journey home was uneventful after that. My wounds healed, though I continued to have nightmares about being under that crush of male bodies angry because I was female. I went off to fly and my brothers and father did not bother me.

They never asked me what had happened at the cave or in the market. The closeness that we'd had at the beginning of the journey was gone. We didn't talk. We didn't share. We didn't laugh. We all just kept to ourselves. And when we reached home, Mama cried and Adoro 5 rejoiced. No one asked about the pink glowing cube of salt we had sold. All the focus was on what it had earned the village and the fact

that it was more than enough to restock the Paper
House while making my family beyond wealthy.

Nevertheless, even after we returned home, Papa
remained . . . changed. At first there were only small
things. He didn't laugh as much. He was quieter. The
very evening we arrived home, the first thing he did
was go with my mother to see the overseer. He spent
the night in the Paper House where the overseer was
recovering. The overseer felt he could only get better
in the presence of books, manuscripts, stories, history, paper. It must have stunk of smoke and char in
those days so soon after the attack. I often wonder
what Papa and the overseer discussed while there. Papa
never shared any of it with me. Papa hadn't shared
anything with me since he'd realized I could control
the salt markets.

After some months, Papa was often out of breath,
staying home with Mama more often than spending
time with his friends and supervising projects. He
never went back to the Paper House, not even to see
the new documents brought in. Not once. I think it
would have pleased him to see that the Paper House
had been rebuilt and stocked better than ever. The
overseer also recovered fully, and he was surlier than
before and even more suspicious of me. I often won-

der if Papa told him about me, what I could do, what I had done.

Weeks later, Papa quietly passed away in his sleep. That creature had pulled something from Papa that day. No one would speak of it, but I knew this was true. Mama grew more distant after that, if Mama was ever anything else. She wrote more often. Other than to greet me occasionally and tell me she loved me, she stopped talking to me. We became like strangers in that house. It was so sad. I no longer saw much of Peter after she married. She didn't even come to see the Paper House restocked. Obi married and I never saw him; his wife wouldn't allow it. I did not go on the salt roads that next year. Neither did my brothers. We did not have to and it would have been dangerous.

I'd felt the call regardless, and it was upsetting. I walked out of the house that day, alone as I was most days at this point. Some women were going to a local market together; Osu-nu women did not shop alone, because it was too dangerous for us. I went with them. It was a five-hour journey by camel. I took Abdul. And it was at this market that I met Idris, a quiet Osu-nu carpenter about my age who was looking for materials for the house he was building himself. He thought

I was beautiful and I thought he was a kind man who was not from my village.

"You're a mysterious woman," he said. "And I love that."

Idris, in turn, was a mysterious man. Behind his quiet and balanced exterior was a man who was recovering from the worst pain of his life. Only months before we met, his village, Adoro 3, had been set upon, not by Okekes who hated Osu-nu, but by Nurus. They'd completely burned down the village Paper House. Many were killed. Idris was living in Adoro 11, squeezed into a small home with several of his family members. He said he was saving up almost all of what he was earning to get back on his feet.

I didn't think twice about saying "yes" when he asked me to marry him. I blurted my mind before I knew I was going to. "I will marry you, Idris. Yes. And let's move far away from my village and the remains of yours." I was shocked by my own words, then pleased by them. This was what I wanted. He'd smiled. It was exactly what he wanted, too.

We married quietly and left that very night, chancing the night roads. Walking into the desert did not scare me at all. Nothing could be as horrible as what I'd already seen on the salt roads and what Idris had seen in his village. Or so I thought back then. Both of us were brave, sad, but also full of hope. There was more to life, we knew. We would create it, we said. We moved to a non-Osu-nu town, close enough to the Seven Rivers Kingdom to see the occasional Nuru, but far enough from the Seven Rivers Kingdom to live freely . . . or so we thought.

We wanted to leave it all behind. I think my mother was glad to see me go, too. My brothers had their families. They probably all quickly forgot about me. Maybe my camel Abdul and my mother's blue-eyed white camel Noor missed me. Maybe. However, I was happy with Idris. I stopped flying. I thought I could be a normal woman with a normal life. I was determined to make it work. But the fact was that my father, back when he was a terrified, recently orphaned boy in that Osu-nu temple, had looked into the Adoro idol's face. He'd spoken to both the goddess Adoro and the goddess Ani. He made . . . a demand. He never told me, but I am sure of it . . .

━━━━━

"Your father demanded for one of his children to be made a sorcerer and seek revenge for the murder of his family and that boy who wanted to marry his sister," Aro finished. "Yet another curse made by an Osu-nu. The result of this one is profound." He looked at the sky and recited, "First, there is great grief, then someone who loves us demands that we become who we must become. And *that* is why you are what you are." He laughed. "Kponyungo."

Najeeba sat back and looked out at the rolling sand dunes. All this had been so long ago, but recounting it to the old sorcerer, after all that had happened, made it feel like yesterday.

"You're almost an old woman now," Aro continued. He laughed, getting up. His garments were caked with sand. He did not slap it off.

"My daughter Onyesonwu has gone," Najeeba said. "Her sacrifice changed the world, but it could not change everything."

"There's no silver bullet that can kill a beast with so many heads." He sighed, walking away. "The work always requires many, never just one."

Najeeba stood up. "Aro, the Okeke people are free of the Nuru now because of my daughter. But the harmony is not perfect. The Osu-nu remain bound to the goddess Adoro. And her Cleanser still walks the land."

"Ahhh, I see now," Aro said, turning back to Najeeba, his interest finally piqued.

"This goes beyond my father's revenge. I want to free my *people*," Najeeba growled, her fists clenched. "Will you train me, sorcerer?"

Aro grinned. "Oh, I most definitely will."